"I want to be alone with you, Cleo"

Cleo sucked in a sharp breath. "Why?" she blurted out before she could stop herself.

"You know why," Bryon said quietly.

"You...you want to have sex with me?" It sounded incredible once she'd said it out loud. Cleo knew she wanted to have sex with him but had never imagined her desire was returned.

"Yes, of course I do."

His casual admission took her breath away. It also angered her.

"I've wanted to have sex with you since thirty seconds after I met you," he added with a rueful smile in his voice, and on his face.

If his earlier admission had taken her breath away, this one left her speechless.

"Are you going to say something?" he queried when she just sat there in stunned silence for several seconds.

"But why?"

"Why?" he echoed thoughtfully. "Perhaps it was because I glimpsed the real you underneath the drab facade."

"The real me?" What on earth was he talking about?

"The one who stared at me for a split second like I was a drink of water after a long and dusty desert trek."

"Oh," she said, embarrassed now.

"There's nothing more desirable," he said, "than a woman who wants you, despite herself."

Marrying a Tycoon

Australia's most eligible tycoons meet their matches at the altar!

Magnate Scott McAllister believes he has the perfect compliant wife, until she defies him! Suddenly he discovers the passionate nature she hides...and is determined to awaken it!

The Magnate's Tempestuous Marriage

Already available!

Tycoon Byron Maddox doesn't do commitment, but shy PA Cleo intrigues him instantly! He wants her in his bed, but will he want her to wear his ring?

The Tycoon's Outrageous Proposal

Available now!

You won't want to miss this dramatic, passionate duet from Miranda Lee!

Miranda Lee

THE TYCOON'S
OUTRAGEOUS PROPOSAL

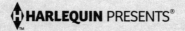

Recycling programs
for this product may
not exist in your area.

ISBN-13: 978-0-373-06093-1

The Tycoon's Outrageous Proposal

First North American Publication 2017

Copyright © 2017 by Miranda Lee

Printed in U.S.A.

www.Harlequin.com

Born and raised in the Australian bush, **Miranda Lee** was boarding-school-educated, and briefly pursued a career in classical music before moving to Sydney and embracing the world of computers. Happily married, with three daughters, she began writing when family commitments kept her at home. She likes to create stories that are believable, modern, fast-paced and sexy. Her interests include meaty sagas, doing word puzzles, gambling and going to the movies.

Books by Miranda Lee

Harlequin Presents

Taken Over by the Billionaire
A Man Without Mercy
Master of Her Virtue
Contract with Consequences
The Man Every Woman Wants
Not a Marrying Man
A Night, A Secret...A Child

Marrying a Tycoon

The Magnate's Tempestuous Marriage

Rich, Ruthless and Renowned

The Italian's Ruthless Seduction
The Billionaire's Ruthless Affair
The Playboy's Ruthless Pursuit

Three Rich Husbands

The Billionaire's Bride of Vengeance
The Billionaire's Bride of Convenience
The Billionaire's Bride of Innocence

Visit the Author Profile page at Harlequin.com for more titles.

CHAPTER ONE

CLEO DIDN'T CRY when she placed the flowers on her husband's grave. She'd cried buckets that morning, once she realised she'd forgotten the anniversary of Martin's death. When she explained to her very concerned boss that she always visited Martin's grave with her mother-in-law on the anniversary of his death, he'd given her the rest of the day off, insisting that she collect Doreen and go.

So here she was with her eyes strangely dry whilst Martin's mother cried buckets instead.

Maybe she was all cried out. Or maybe—just maybe—she'd finished with grieving. She'd loved Martin. In the end. And in the beginning. But there'd been that awful time in the middle when she hadn't loved him at all. Hard to stay in love with a man who tried to run every aspect of your life, from where you worked to what you wore and who your friends were. At home, it had been just as bad. From the day they were married, Martin took control of the money, paid all the bills, and made all the decisions.

Her own fault, of course. At first, she'd liked his 'take control' attitude, had thought it manly. His decisiveness had appealed to her own lack of confidence and maturity. She'd been engaged at twenty, married at twenty-one. Just a baby, really, in more ways than one.

But all babies eventually grew up, and she'd come to see how stifling it was being married to a man who wanted you to stay totally dependent on him, who wouldn't even let you have a baby until the mortgage was totally paid off so he could afford for you to be a full-time stay-at-home mother, a prospect that hadn't appealed to Cleo. She'd liked her job in the marketing section of McAllister Mines, despite it having been chosen for her by Martin, solely because he'd worked there in the accounts division.

Cleo had made the momentous decision to leave Martin on the very day when he'd told her that he'd been diagnosed with cancer, a particularly aggressive melanoma, which the doctor had warned might not be curable.

It had turned out it wasn't. But it had taken Martin two long years to die, during which time Cleo had learned to love him again. How brave he'd been during that terrible time. And how sorry for what he'd put her through during their marriage. Oh, yes, he knew exactly what he'd been doing all along; had known it was wrong, but said he couldn't seem to help himself. Apparently, his father had treated his mother the same way, and consequently it was all he'd known as a model for marriage. In Cleo's eyes it was no excuse, but it was at least an explanation for his behaviour.

His debilitating illness forced him to give up his controlling nature, gradually relying on Cleo to do everything for him. The balance of power shifted substantially, giving Cleo a new confidence in her ability to cope once Martin died, which soon became inevitable, once the cancer spread to his brain. She'd thought she'd be relieved when he passed away, and she was, in a way. But not long after, she'd become very depressed. If it hadn't been for the boss of McAllister Mines promoting her to the challenging position of his PA, she wasn't sure what might have become of her. She'd always suffered from depression, ever since her parents had been killed in a car accident when she was a teenager, leaving her to be raised by her paternal grandparents who were way too old—and way too old-fashioned—to know what a thirteen-year-old girl needed.

Thinking of her sad teenage years sparked the tears that had been absent up until then.

Doreen saw them and came over to link arms with her. 'Now, now, love,' she said, dabbing at her own tears with a wad of tissues. 'We shouldn't be sad. He's not in pain any longer. He's at peace now.'

'Yes,' was all Cleo could think of to say. She could hardly tell Martin's mother that she was crying for herself, not Martin.

'Maybe you shouldn't do this any more, Cleo,' Doreen added. 'It's been three years, and it's not always good to dwell on the past. You're still a young woman. You should be out there, dating.'

'Dating?' Cleo could not have been more surprised if Doreen had said fishing. Cleo hated fishing. Martin, however, had loved it, and had insisted she go along with him, even on their honeymoon.

'You don't have to sound so shocked,' Doreen said.

'And who, precisely, do you envisage me dating?'

Doreen shrugged. 'You must meet plenty of attractive men in the course of your work.'

'Actually, I don't. If they are even marginally attractive, they're always married. Besides, I'm not interested in dating.'

'Why not?'

Cleo could hardly tell her mother-in-law that her son had killed off any interest she'd had in sex. She'd quite liked it, to begin with. But her hormones had gone into hibernation once they were married, once he started telling her what to do and how to do it, blaming *her* when she didn't come, forcing her to start faking her climaxes, just to get some peace. It had been a relief when chemo affected Martin's testosterone levels. Sex was the last thing on his mind when he was fighting for his life, and without the toxic effect of their missing physical connection, Cleo found she could be genuinely affectionate with her husband. She'd been holding his hand and telling him how much she loved him when he died.

And it had been true. She *had* loved him. But the damage had been done by then. She never looked at a man these days and thought of sex. She didn't want it, dream of it, or crave it. So naturally, she never entertained the thought of dating, or getting married again. Because marriage meant sex; it meant having to consider a man's wishes.

'I don't want to date,' Cleo said at last. 'And I definitely don't want to get married again.'

Doreen nodded, as though she understood perfectly.

She must have seen that her son was a chip off the old block. If Cleo had been emotionally abused in her marriage, then so had Doreen. Damaged, they were. Both of them.

Cleo looked at her mother-in-law and thought it was a shame. Doreen was still young, only fifty-two, and still slim and attractive. *She* should be the one getting out and dating. There had to be some nice men left in the world. Surely.

Of course there were, Cleo conceded, thinking of her boss. Scott was a wonderful man. Kind. Caring. A good husband. When he wasn't being stupid, that was. Cleo could not believe how close he and Sarah had come to breaking up. Still, all was right in their world again now, which was a relief. Last week had been a nightmare!

She shook her head and sighed wearily.

'I think we should go home,' Doreen said gently, obviously misinterpreting that sigh.

Cleo smiled at the woman who was more than a mother-in-law these days. She was her best friend, having moved in to help Cleo with Martin towards the end of his illness…and never leaving. Widowed just before Cleo had met Martin, Doreen had never owned a house with her husband, so after Martin died, Cleo had asked Doreen to move in with her permanently. She'd jumped at the chance and neither woman had ever regretted it.

Thanks to Martin's taking out enough life insurance to cover the mortgage, Cleo owned her house in Leichardt, an inner western suburb where the value of properties had skyrocketed lately, due to its proximity to Sydney's Central Business District. It wasn't a large house, and it was a little run-down, but, still, it was hers and it meant independence and freedom.

'Good idea,' Cleo returned and started walking back to the car park. 'What's on TV tonight?'

'Not much,' Doreen replied. 'We could watch one of the movies I put in the planner.'

'Okay,' Cleo said, always happy to watch a movie. 'But I hope it's not a miserable one,' she added. 'I can't stand those dreary issue movies.' She wanted to be entertained, not depressed.

Before Doreen could comment, Cleo's phone rang, and she rifled in her handbag to retrieve it. It was Scott, as she suspected. Not many other people ever rang her, except scam callers. And they always waited until she was home in the evening, cooking dinner.

'It's my boss,' she said, putting her phone up to her ear with one hand whilst she handed Doreen her car keys with the other. 'I have to take this. You go back to the car. I won't be long. Scott! What's up?' She hoped everything was still good with his wife.

'Nothing drastic,' he replied. 'Sorry to intrude on your afternoon off. Everything go all right with the flowers?'

'Oh, yes. Fine.' Cleo's conscience pricked that her visit to the cemetery was already out of her mind.

'Good. Just thought I should let you know I've decided to take Sarah away to Phuket on a second honeymoon.'

'Oh, Scott, what a wonderful idea! When?'

'That's why I'm ringing you. We're leaving tomorrow afternoon.'

'Tomorrow!'

'Yep. And we'll be gone for two weeks.'

'But you've got an appointment with Byron Maddox at lunchtime this Wednesday,' she reminded him. With the price of minerals plummeting recently—and that infernal nickel refinery a virtual money pit—McAllister Mines was in financial trouble. Scott had asked her to find him a potential partner with sufficient funds to improve his cash flow and take the load off him. *And* his marriage.

Byron Maddox had been first cab off the rank. Actually, the only one she could find on short notice who had enough money to qualify, Scott having asked Cleo to find him an Australian investor this time.

'I know,' Scott said, not sounding at all worried. 'I thought you could stand in for me.'

'He's not going to be happy with that, Scott. It's you he wants to see, not me.'

'Not necessarily. He just wants the heads up on the business at this early stage. You know as much about McAllister Mines as I do.'

'That's very flattering but not true.'

'Don't underestimate yourself, Cleo. I have every confidence in you.'

Good Lord, he was going to go off and drop her right in it, wasn't he? Cleo knew full well that she wasn't at her best dealing one-on-one with a man like Byron Maddox. She could handle being Scott's assistant during business meetings, but her social skills faltered badly when she was left on her own with men who expected every female they dealt with to flirt and flatter them inordinately.

Cleo would never be a flirt or a flatterer. Neither was she ingratiating or coy or submissive. Though there'd been a time when she'd been guilty of the latter. These days, she was a very up-front, straight-down-the-line girl who found it impossible to use feminine wiles when doing business. This made her popular with wives—if there *were* wives—but not with their spouses. And certainly not with the bachelor businessmen she'd come across.

Cleo winced at the thought of going—*alone*—to a business lunch with Byron Maddox.

'I'll do my best,' she told Scott with resignation in her voice. 'But please don't expect miracles.'

'Like I said, Cleo, I have every confidence in you. Now I have to ring Harvey as well as all my section managers and let them know that you're in charge for the next two weeks. Then I really have to go home. Sarah's in a flap about being ready in time. Look, I probably won't see you at all tomorrow so I'm saying my goodbyes now.'

'Do you want me to call you after the meeting with Maddox?' she asked before he could escape.

'Absolutely. Have to go, Cleo. Good luck.'

And he was gone.

Cleo sucked in a deep breath then let it out slowly as she walked back to the car. She didn't begrudge Scott his happiness. She also didn't mind being in charge of the office for a couple of weeks. But she certainly wasn't looking forward to Wednesday.

'What did your boss want?' Doreen asked as she climbed in behind the steering wheel. 'You look worried.'

Cleo sighed as she gunned the engine. She was worried. Very worried indeed.

CHAPTER TWO

WHO WOULD HAVE thought that getting married would prove so difficult?

Byron pondered this surprising reality as he practised his putting on the smooth grey carpet that covered the floor of his spacious office.

One would have thought that a highly eligible bachelor of his wealth and looks would have found little trouble in securing himself a bride.

Not so, it seemed!

After Byron cut business ties with his media mogul father five years ago, he returned home to Sydney with two missions in mind. First, to establish his own successful investment company; second, to marry and enjoy the same happy family life his father had finally found. He'd achieved his first goal but so far had failed spectacularly with the second.

It wasn't that Byron hadn't tried. He'd actually been engaged twice during the last two years, both of his fiancées having been exceptionally beautiful young women who were very keen to wed the only son and heir of the Maddox Media Empire.

Unfortunately, neither relationship had gone the distance from engagement to the altar. The fact it had been *his* decision both times didn't alter his disappointment. Plus, it wasn't cheap to dispose of an eager fiancée quietly when you were as rich as he was. But Byron didn't regret either break-up, not once he realised he could not spend the rest of his life with a woman he no longer loved, or perhaps never had loved in the first place.

Within a few short weeks of his putting a ring on each woman's finger, his rose-coloured glasses had fallen off and he'd seen them for what they were. Not true loves at all, but vain, ambitious women who wanted the *status* of being married to him more than they wanted to actually be married to him.

True love, Byron decided as he lined up his next putt, was a rare commodity, though his father seemed to have been lucky second time around. During his recent visit to New York for his new half-sister's christening, Byron had been impressed with Alexandra's devotion to her husband. But maybe he was deluding himself on that score. Lloyd Maddox was, after all, one of the richest and most powerful men in the world. How would he ever know if a woman loved him, or his money?

Byron swore when his putt was as unsuccessful as all the others, the ball hitting the side of the practice chute. Frustrated, he strode over to throw open his office door.

'Grace!' he called out to his PA. 'Could you spare a moment or two? I need your advice on something.' Grace and her husband were regular golfers; perhaps she could spot what he was doing wrong.

'I hope you haven't forgotten that you have to be ready

for a business luncheon with Cleo Shelton in fifteen minutes,' Grace reminded him as she walked in, balefully eyeing the golf club in his hand, plus his rolled-up shirt sleeves.

A swift glance at the gold Rolex on his wrist showed that it was a quarter past twelve. 'Hell on earth,' he muttered. 'Where has the time gone this morning?'

'They say time flies when you're having fun,' Grace offered.

'Fun! Golf's not fun. It's sheer bloody torture. I have to endure eighteen holes with the owner of Fantasy Productions this Friday. The man plays off scratch. If I don't fix my putting he'll slaughter me.'

It irritated Byron that he had been so far unable to master golf. At school, he'd excelled at cricket, tennis, swimming and rugby.

Grace smiled. 'I can imagine,' she said as she followed him into his office. 'But look on the bright side. If you let Blake Randall humiliate you on the golf course, he'll be more inclined to agree to bigger investment from you in his next movie. Fantasy Productions is on a roll, especially since they snapped up that handsome young hunk straight out of NIDA and made him a star.'

She was right. Byron knew she was right. Grace was always right. In her late forties, Grace had worked for the CEO of a merchant bank before Byron had headhunted her five years ago.

Byron threw Grace a droll look. 'Just tell me what I'm doing wrong here, please.'

Byron lined himself up for another putt. He took his time, aimed, struck the ball. And missed again.

His four-letter swear word did not faze Grace one bit.

'Okay,' he grumped. 'What am I doing wrong?'

'Only two things that I could see on such a short sample. First, your feet aren't straight. Your left toes are in front of your right. Second, you're moving your hips during your backstroke. You have to keep still, and swing your shoulders back and forth in a gentle pendulum motion when you putt, not attack the ball like you would on the fairway.'

Byron frowned, then tried again, following Grace's instructions with perfect concentration. The ball rolled smoothly along the carpet, then right up the centre of the chute and into the plastic cup.

'See?' Grace said smugly when Byron lifted an amazed face to her. 'But watch it. Keep doing that and you might win on Friday.'

'Heaven forbid,' he said, grinning his delight at the thought.

'Now, I think you should put your putter away,' Grace advised. 'Your visitor will be here shortly. Cleo doesn't strike me as the sort of woman to be late. Best roll down your sleeves and put your jacket on as well. First impressions, you know.'

Byron snorted. 'It's not me who has to do the impressing. I'm still quite annoyed that McAllister has sent a secretary in his place whilst he swans off on holidays.'

'Cleo Shelton's a lot more than a secretary, Byron,' Grace chided. 'From what I've gleaned on the grapevine, she's Scott McAllister's deputy, not just his assistant. I wouldn't underestimate her if I were you. Neither would

I get on her bad side if you're seriously considering a partnership in McAllister Mines.'

He wasn't. Not really. They'd sought him out, not the other way around. It was hardly the right time to be investing in the mining industry. He'd agreed to the meeting more out of curiosity than genuine interest.

'And for your information,' Grace added, 'Cleo's boss hasn't just swanned off on any old holiday. He's taken his wife on a second honeymoon after they experienced some kind of crisis in their marriage.'

Byron was constantly amazed at how much inside knowledge Grace managed to acquire about the people he did business with. Not that he was complaining; knowledge was power. He wondered what their marital crisis had involved. Another man perhaps?

Byron had met McAllister and his wife once at the spring racing carnival last year. Whilst *he'd* not been anything to write home about, *she'd* been a real looker, the sort of girl men would pursue, married or not. Such a thought reminded Byron that he had made a narrow escape in not marrying either of his fiancées. They'd been beautiful as well. Next time, he'd pick a girl who didn't stop traffic. Someone only marginally attractive. Someone with brains. God, but he couldn't bear the thought of a wife without brains. Whilst his previous fiancées had not been dumb, they'd been shallow thinkers. And eventually, dead boring.

Boring was the ultimate sin in Byron's opinion.

'So when will McAllister be back?' he asked as he rolled down his shirt sleeves and did up the buttons.

'Cleo said two weeks. She wasn't sure of the exact

date and time of his return. His going away was rather…
spontaneous.'

Byron nodded, then walked around and lifted his suit
jacket off the back of his chair.

'Try not to be patronising with Cleo,' Grace advised.

Byron scowled as he put on his jacket. 'I am never
patronising.'

'Yes, you are. When you think you're cleverer than
the person you're with.'

'Only when they really are stupid. I can't abide stupid people.'

Grace smiled. 'I've rather gathered that. But Cleo
doesn't come across as at all stupid.'

'I'll be the judge of that. How old is she, do you know?'

'My guess would be somewhere between thirty and
forty, given her position in the company.'

'That narrows it down,' he said with a wry laugh.

'Hopefully, she won't be a blonde with false eyelashes
and enhanced breasts.'

Byron recognised a jibe when he heard one. Both his
fiancées had been blonde, with eyelashes and breasts that
defied reality. His sigh demonstrated how foolish he felt
now that he'd ever been taken in by them.

'Indeed,' he agreed. 'Well, show her in when she ar-
rives and I'll do my best to be charming and not patronising. What time did you make our reservation for?'

'One o'clock.'

'Perfect.'

CHAPTER THREE

THE SHOWER CAME out of the blue, just as Cleo was crossing the road at the intersection of Elizabeth and King Streets. Not a light drizzle but a real dumping. By the time she found shelter under the shop awnings on the other side, Cleo was very wet indeed.

'Damn and blast,' she muttered under her breath as she brushed the heavy droplets off her shoulders then smoothed back her damp hair. 'Should have caught a taxi.'

The trouble was that catching taxis in the CBD of Sydney often promised a very slow ride, construction on the new light rail network having caused havoc with the traffic. So Cleo had set off in plenty of time to walk the four blocks from the building where she worked down to the skyscraper that housed BM Enterprises. Her appointment was for twelve-thirty, where she was having a short meeting with Byron Maddox in his office before enjoying a long business lunch with him.

Or, at least she assumed it would be long. Cleo had found, over the time she'd been Scott's PA, that successful men like Maddox liked to linger over their business lunches whilst they plied their dinner guests with bottles of the very best wine, playing one-upmanship to the hilt. She'd noticed that the smartest of them didn't drink all that much themselves, taking advantage of their guests' sozzled states to ferret out facts that a more sober brain wouldn't have let slip.

Scott had never fallen for that trick. He was too canny for that. Neither did he ever do business that way himself. He was a man of the utmost integrity and honesty in all his dealings with others. He also actually *cared* about his employees. Of course, Scott hadn't been brought up and trained by the most ruthless business brain in the world. Cleo was under no illusions that, despite his reputation, Byron Maddox was as cunning and as ruthless as his father. She had no intention of falling victim to any of his ploys. Cleo had a very important mission on her plate today.

Almost a mission impossible, she conceded as she hurried down the street. It wasn't going to be easy to persuade the billionaire owner of BM Enterprises that, despite the economic climate in the mining world today, it was the perfect time for him to become a partner in McAllister Mines. Because without his partnership—and buckets of his money—McAllister Mines was headed for big trouble. Scott had been way too distracted lately to realise how serious things were, but Cleo had her finger on the pulse. If she didn't pull off this coup, the company she loved was headed for dire financial trouble.

In light of her mission, Cleo had chosen her clothes carefully that morning. Nothing sexy—not that she ever dressed sexy. The idea was ludicrous, given she had no interest in attracting men. She'd finally selected her most professional, severely tailored black trouser suit, teaming it with a crisp white shirt and low-heeled black pumps. Her thick and somewhat wayward dark hair she'd tied back into a tight bun at the nape of her neck. A fortuitous choice, now that her hair was wet. If she'd left her hair down she would have looked like a drowned rat. Hopefully, by the time she reached her destination, she would have dried out somewhat.

However, it was not to be. She greeted her reflection in the mirror of the powder room with little pleasure, but, not being vain, she only cared that she presented a professional image to Mr Maddox.

'Not too bad,' she reassured her reflection. Thank heavens she never wore make-up, otherwise she might have had to use up valuable minutes doing an emergency repair job. Cleo did so hate being late for appointments, a hangover from being brought up by her very elderly grandparents who considered punctuality one of the most important virtues. That, along with cleanliness, loyalty, honesty and modesty.

After Cleo dried her briefcase with some paper towels, she headed out to find the lifts. They were at the back of the cavernous foyer behind a huge cement sculpture, which Cleo thought was ridiculously large and downright ugly. She liked art to be sensible and pleasing to the eye, again the result of being raised by people who thought modern art was a con.

'Utter rubbish,' her grandfather had snorted whenever he saw a modern painting. 'Any child in kindergarten could have done just as well.'

Cleo smiled at the thought. Grandpa had been a character; her grandma, not so much. She'd been the sort of woman who'd found it hard to show love. Not a hugger, that was for sure.

Once Cleo found a lift that wasn't full, she pressed the button for the thirty-ninth floor, and when the doors opened she entered a reception area that was so glamorous it was hard not to blink, or to stare.

Black marble-tiled floors. White Italian leather lounge furniture. Glass coffee and side-tables. Even a chandelier overhead, for pity's sake. But the finishing touch was the stylishly curved, glass reception desk that framed a receptionist who was straight out of a Hollywood casting. Possibly thirtyish, she was glamour personified with her ash-blonde hair styled into a shoulder-length bob, her attractive face perfectly made up. Her lipstick was a bright red gloss, highlighting her full lips and contrasting vibrantly with her expensive-looking white woollen dress. Her legs were visible underneath the desk. They were long and shapely, crossed at the knees and shod in the highest of high heels.

Suddenly, Cleo felt like a fish out of water in her ugly pants suit and plain white shirt. Her eyes dropped to her boring black pumps and her even more boring black briefcase. Maybe she'd made a mistake dressing the way she had for a meeting with Byron Maddox. She should have known that the playboy billionaire liked women looking as if they had stepped straight out of a beauty salon. She'd checked him out on the Internet, hadn't she? But then, even had she wanted to, she wouldn't have known how to doll herself up like this girl. She didn't have the looks, the clothes, nor any sexy shoes.

'May I help you?' the girl asked with that slightly superior manner that, in Cleo's experience, beautiful girls sometimes adopted with their less attractive sisters.

Cleo shrugged off the momentary temptation to let it affect her, smiling at the girl and informing her that she had an appointment with Mr Maddox at twelve-thirty.

That changed the girl's snooty attitude.

'Oh,' she said, uncrossing her legs and standing up straight away. But she did frown as she gave Cleo a second once-over, as though wondering what on earth someone like her was doing going out to lunch with her very handsome bachelor-of-the-year boss.

It was an undermining experience to be on the end of such a critical scrutiny. Scott didn't care what she looked like, as long as she did her work. Not that she didn't always look neat and tidy. She just didn't know anything about fashion, but even she knew her working wardrobe was very bland.

And, let's face it, Cleo, boring.

'This way, please,' the girl said crisply, before taking off down a nearby hallway, her hips swinging as she walked.

Following her was an education, Cleo thought, though she doubted she could walk so confidently in six-inch heels. She'd never worn high heels at all after meeting Martin, because he was short and didn't like her to tower over him. Then, after his death, she didn't care enough to dress differently. By then she was used to low heels, anyway. They were way more practical and comfortable.

Somehow, however, being practical and comfortable didn't cut it today. For a crushing moment, Cleo wished she were sashaying into this meeting looking elegant and glamorous, and done up to the nines. But then she pulled herself together and told herself not to be so silly. Byron Maddox was a clever businessman, above all else. He wouldn't really care what she looked like, as long as she knew her stuff. And at least in that she was confident.

This last thought reassured her so that when she was shown into Grace's office, Cleo felt reasonably composed. Though seeing Grace in the flesh didn't exactly help her confidence. Maddox's PA was considerably older than his receptionist—possibly in her late forties—but still very attractive and groomed within an inch of her life. A blonde too. Clearly, Byron Maddox preferred blondes. His former fiancées had both been blondes. Cleo had seen their photos on the Internet.

Grace's manner, however, was nothing like the receptionist's. She was warm and welcoming, with not a hint of disapproval over Cleo's appearance. If anything, she seemed to approve of how Cleo looked, which was a relief.

'I knew you wouldn't be late,' she said with a ready smile.

'I almost was,' Cleo returned. 'I got caught in a sun shower on the way over and had to make a side trip to the ladies' before coming up. I'm afraid my hair is still damp,' she added, patting it with her right hand.

'You *walked* all the way here?' Grace said, sounding surprised.

Cleo nodded. 'Faster than a taxi these days.'

The woman's eyes dropped to Cleo's shoes, then to her own. They had stiletto heels, though not as high as the receptionist's.

'I can never walk far in these shoes,' Grace said. 'Yours are way more sensible. But enough of this chit-chat. Byron's anxious to meet you.'

Cleo's stomach tightened as she was ushered over to the door that clearly led into Byron Maddox's inner sanctum. She wasn't usually given to nervous anxiety. Since Martin's death, nothing much fazed her any more. Watching your husband die slowly of cancer did something to your emotions. She sometimes envied Scott's wife, Sarah, who had a warm, bubbly personality. Cleo suspected that most people *she* met and dealt with found her distant, and cold. Scott really should be the one to be here doing this, not her.

Oh, well, she thought resignedly as Grace knocked on the door. *What will be, will be.*

'Come in,' a male voice invited. It was a pleasant enough voice. Not too deep or too threatening. She disliked bosses who barked at their employees, especially their PAs. But, of course, Byron Maddox would not be a barker. He'd be a charmer. Cleo had read up about him. Underneath the charm, however, would lie the mind of a man who'd built his own successful company in five short years. She had to be careful not to underestimate him. He might have the look of a playboy—and the life-style—but he was sure to be a chip off the old block. No one would dare underestimate Lloyd Maddox. Colleagues and enemies had done so in the past at their peril.

Or so she'd read in an article written by a journalist in *Forbes* magazine.

Grace opened the door. 'Cleo's here,' she said in a highly natural and familiar manner, which boded well. Clearly, she wasn't afraid of her boss. Cleo's own tension eased somewhat.

She stepped into an office that would have done a Hollywood producer proud. Everything was very spacious, very expensive and very male, from the thick sable-coloured carpet to the book-lined walls and the built-in drinks cabinet. Two chocolate-brown chesterfields flanked the floor-to-ceiling plate-glass window that stretched along the far wall and provided an uninterrupted view of Sydney and the harbour, with all its splendid icons. Stretched in front of this window was a huge desk, made in a rich dark wood, behind which sat Byron Maddox in a high-backed brown leather swivel chair.

He rose immediately after Grace retreated and closed the door, thus giving Cleo a complete view of his attractions. Which were considerable.

Cleo already knew he was a handsome man, a tall, fair-haired god with the kind of even facial features and good bone structure that made male models and movie stars so photogenic. But in the flesh, he was more than that. Maybe it was his sparkling blue eyes, or his sexy mouth, or his tall, broad-shouldered frame, which was superbly housed in the type of business suit that screamed Italian tailoring. His effect on Cleo was instantaneous and quite startling. Her female hormones—which she'd believed dead and buried—leapt into life, threatening to bring an unwelcome and humiliating heat to her neck and face.

Luckily, she managed to keep her reaction restricted to just a racing heartbeat and a squishy feeling in her stomach, but it was the disorientating effect on her brain that rattled her the most. She could hardly think straight!

Cleo was still out of kilter when he said something in greeting, then reached out his hand to shake hers, accompanying the gesture with a winning smile that showed perfect white teeth. Her own returning smile felt robotic, her teeth clamped tightly together as the corners of her mouth lifted only slightly. She must have put her own hand out as well, because suddenly it was encased within the warmth of his, his other hand reaching to cover their handshake at the same time, keeping her fingers solidly captive in his clasp.

It was possibly a well-practised ploy, Cleo was to think later—after her brain started working again— but it worked brilliantly at the time, making her warm to him even further as well as want him in a way she'd never wanted a man before.

This last appalling thought snapped her out of her uncharacteristically muddled state of mind. How could she *possibly* want Byron Maddox like that? And so *quickly*? It had taken her weeks to go to bed with Martin. And she'd been deeply in love with him. Yet within seconds of meeting Byron Maddox all she could think about was how it would feel to lie naked in his arms, to have his mouth explore every part of her.

Cleo was shocked by her desires. He'd be good in

bed, she just knew it. After all, he'd had plenty of practice. Martin had been a virgin when they met, as had she. They'd both been highly embarrassed after their first fumbling attempts at sex. They'd worked things out eventually and she'd quite enjoyed herself at the beginning of their relationship. But not all the time. No, definitely not all the time.

Cleo stared into Byron Maddox's blue eyes with the certainty that she would enjoy herself every time with this man.

But it was all just fantasy, she knew, using her hard-won strength of character to control her rampant desires and face reality. Cleo knew full well that she would never have the opportunity to find out what kind of lover Byron Maddox was. She was not the sort of woman this bachelor playboy took to bed. She wasn't blonde, or beautiful, or sexy. She was a very ordinary brunette with no fashion sense and zero sex appeal.

Well, that was life, she supposed. *Her* life, anyway. It was perverse, however, that after not caring about men or sex since Martin's death, the one man she found fascinating in that regard was totally out of her reach.

Which was just as well, she thought, as she carefully extracted her hand from his and found her best business face. She already had a difficult mission to achieve today with this man. She didn't need the distraction of trying to seduce him as well—the ridiculous impossibility of *that* mission evoked a wild urge to laugh. She smothered the impulse much more easily than she was smothering her highly unwanted cravings.

'I am so sorry Scott wasn't able to keep his appointment with you,' she said with cool politeness. 'Hopefully, I can tell you everything you need to know over lunch.'

Byron doubted it. Because he wanted to know quite a lot. Not just about McAllister Mines but about Cleo Shelton, PA extraordinaire. And a woman of contradictions.

Byron was usually a good judge of females but this one had him stumped. When she'd first walked in he'd been taken aback by her appearance. Dull was his initial thought. Dull and boring. He *hated* boring. He also hated black pant suits and drab black pumps and severe, scraped-back hairstyles. He liked women to look like women.

But when he came closer to her, he'd seen she wasn't as plain as he'd originally thought. Or as old. No more than thirty. She had lovely unlined olive skin and fine dark eyes. Her mouth was a little wide but her lips were nicely shaped. It was her lack of lipstick—or any make-up at all—that gave a colourless first impression. Her hairdo did little for her as well. Talk about unflattering!

He hadn't known what to make of her, especially when he saw the look she gave him as he walked towards her. For a few seconds her eyes had glittered the way a girl's eyes glittered when sexual attraction raised its delightful head. When he'd shaken her hand, he'd felt heat in her palm, plus a slight quivering up her arm. And oddly, he'd responded in kind, suddenly finding his own hormones sparking as well. He'd liked the way she'd stared at him. Liked it a lot, his sexually charged imagination filling with images of how she would look without those dreadful clothes on, her mouth gasping wide with pleasure.

But then abruptly, everything changed. She pulled her hand away and, when she spoke, her voice was as cool as her eyes. Given the way she was dressed, he didn't believe she was playing hard to get. She was no seductress. Byron knew, however, that he hadn't made a mistake in his assessment of her initial attraction to him. For some reason, she was pulling back from it, hiding it away as though it didn't exist.

It was then that he noticed the simple gold wedding band on her left hand.

Byron swore in his head. So *that* was the reason. Admirable, but still annoying. He'd been looking forward to finding out more about her, to peeling back the layers of her enigmatic personality and discovering exactly what made her tick.

Not much point now. Byron only enjoyed that kind of conversation if it led to bed.

Which it still could do… She might be separated, or divorced. Women didn't always get rid of their wedding rings. And there was no engagement ring, he noted with a surge of excitement.

Byron's somewhat desperate reasoning frustrated him. What in hell did it matter? He didn't do married women, no matter how unhappy they were. He also wasn't partial to divorcees—too much emotional baggage. Besides, he was in search of a wife, not an affair.

Back to the business at hand!

'I'm not absolutely sure that mining is my cup of tea,' he said matter-of-factly. 'But I'd like to hear what you have to say, Cleo. It will be up to you to convince me over lunch of the benefits of putting my money into McAllister Mines. Do you mind me calling you Cleo?' he added after seeing her flinch slightly at his familiarity.

'Whatever you prefer,' she returned with a stiff little smile.

'Good. And you must call me Byron. And speaking of lunch,' he went on, glancing at his watch, 'perhaps we should go downstairs. There's an excellent restaurant in this building, on the thirtieth floor. Our reservation isn't until one but it won't matter if we're early. We could have a drink or two. You don't have to drive home, do you?'

'No. I always catch the train.'

'Excellent.'

'What about you?'

'I own the penthouse in this building.'

CHAPTER FOUR

How PREDICTABLE, CLEO thought ruefully as he cupped her left elbow and steered her from his office. A penthouse pad to go with his penthouse lifestyle.

Still, Byron Maddox was *exactly* as she had expected. A charmer, who, despite his obvious intelligence and business acumen, lived the life of a playboy. Cleo wondered why he had bothered to get engaged those two times. Neither engagement had lasted long, and each time the press had had a field-day, which was why she'd been able to find so many articles about him on the Internet.

What Cleo hadn't expected, however, was that she would fall victim to his charm. Or was it just his looks that had fired up her female hormones? He was, after all, exceptionally handsome.

Yes, possibly it was just that. She wouldn't be the first girl to lose her head over Byron Maddox. Though she was hardly a girl. She was twenty-nine, for pity's sake. Not that Cleo had any intention of actually losing her head over him. Still, it was proving awfully hard not to react to the touch of his hand at her elbow, not to freeze in fear or to shiver in ecstasy, making her wonder what it would feel like to have those long, elegant fingers on other parts of her body. And *in* other parts of her body.

Stop it!

Cleo carefully scooped in a deep breath, then let it out slowly.

'Have a good lunch,' Grace said jauntily as Byron guided Cleo past his PA's desk.

'Indeed we will,' Byron replied cheerfully.

Cleo smiled through gritted teeth.

The restaurant was called Thirty—named, no doubt, after the floor it was on.

Cleo liked its spacious feel and unfussy decor, the floors done in large, pale grey tiles; the tables were covered with dark grey linen tablecloths and set with elegant cutlery and glasses. The white walls were broken up by a multitude of long rectangular windows, the high ceiling painted black with subtle recessed lighting. There was a black circular bar in the centre of the room, which wasn't too glitzy.

They were led past the bar to a far table set for two—but which would have accommodated four guests—situated next to a window that had a view of the botanical gardens, the Opera House and the harbour beyond. The waiter assigned to look after them was named André and was quick to pull out Cleo's chair for her. Byron seated himself opposite and immediately ordered cocktails for them both without consulting the drinks menu, or her.

Now, if anything was certain to annoy Cleo—as well as dampen any unwanted desires—it was a man who didn't consult. She had little appreciation of chauvinism; of men who thought they knew better than women.

There'd been a time when she'd been happy to play the compliant little woman, deferring to Martin in all matters. But those days had long passed. Any man these days who dared to make decisions for her did so at his peril. Only the fact that she was supposed to be winning this man over for her boss had her holding her tongue.

But she suspected already that Byron Maddox was not a suitable investor for McAllister Mines. Scott wanted a hands-on partner, not just a money man; someone to take some of the day-to-day load off him, leaving him more time for his wife and future family. Sarah had confided to her before she left on their second honeymoon yesterday that she was pregnant, news that had made Cleo very happy indeed. She'd been seriously worried about their marriage for a while. Scott had been over the moon, of course. What a lovely genuine man he was.

'I possibly should have asked you what drink you preferred,' Byron said, interrupting her train of thought. 'But the cocktails here are to die for and I wanted you to experience at least one.'

'How thoughtful of you,' she said, gritting her teeth.

'So,' he said, picking up the two leather-encased menus sitting in the centre of the table, handing her one then opening the other. 'What do you fancy, Cleo?'

Still you, she conceded with a smothered sigh.

She could hardly take her eyes off him. But she did, dropping her gaze to the menu.

'The seafood here is very good,' he said. 'But so are the steaks. Do you want an entrée to begin with? I would recommend the scallops, if you like seafood.'

Cleo's appetite had fled since she was not used to being affected like this by a man. Her thoughts kept straying into strange territory. The temptation to flirt was extreme, and very perturbing. It had rattled her.

Her stomach contracted as she stared blankly at the menu. 'I'm honestly not very hungry,' she admitted at last. 'I haven't been sleeping all that well lately. Things have been rather hectic at work. And stressful,' she added.

When Cleo glanced up she was surprised to see a spark of genuine sympathy in those sexy blue eyes of his.

'You poor thing,' he said, his kind words rattling her even further. 'Scott did dump you in it, going away suddenly like that when his business was in trouble. But if you're not sleeping then you definitely need to eat,' he went on cheerfully. 'Unless, of course, you're so catatonic that you'll fall asleep with your head in the soup.'

His smile—plus his good humour—bewitched her even more than his looks. Before she knew it, she found herself smiling back at him.

'I'm not that bad. But my head is a little fuzzy.'

He laughed. 'It's going to be even fuzzier once you get the cocktail I ordered into you. When I said it was to die for, I wasn't just talking about the taste. The alcoholic content is off the Richter scale. Ah, here it is.'

It was, as he'd warned her, deadly. But delicious. And decadent. And not designed to dampen desire.

On the plus side, it did relax her, at the same time rendering her a little reckless. She didn't flirt with him exactly. But she let him order the food for her, as well as a bottle of white wine. Before she knew it, she was blurt-

ing out all the pitfalls besetting the mining industry at
the moment. By the time dessert arrived—a light dish
of fresh tropical fruits topped with a mango-flavoured
yoghurt—Cleo realised suddenly how unwise she'd been
and did her best to redress the situation.

'Of course, things will turn around eventually,' she
told a seemingly fascinated Byron. 'The prices of iron
ore will go back up, as will coal and most of the other
minerals. It's just a matter of time.'

'What about Scott's nickel refinery?' he asked. 'I
heard that it was on the point of bankruptcy.'

Cleo knew there was no saving the refinery. Not at
the moment. But to say so would be the kiss of death to
any potential investor in McAllister Mines. As much as
she didn't think Byron was the right man for the role of
Scott's business partner, neither did she want to be re-
sponsible for killing off his interest entirely.

'The refinery is in deep trouble, no doubt about that,'
she admitted. 'But it's not bankrupt.' Not yet, anyway.

'Hmm,' he said. 'I don't like to be a doubting Thomas,
Cleo, but I won't take your word for that. Before I com-
mit myself to any kind of investment, I always have it
thoroughly investigated. Do you have any objections to
me sending my accountant over to check your books?'

Cleo was not surprised by the request. It was a perfectly reasonable one, which Scott had anticipated before he left. 'That will be fine,' she said, relieved that
the diamond mine was doing well at least. *And* the two
gold mines Scott owned. The rest of McAllister Mines
were borderline, the prices for iron ore, coal and cobalt
at an all-time low.

'Good,' Byron said. 'I'll send him over first thing tomorrow morning. Meanwhile, I'd like to go and inspect the refinery for myself.'

Now *that* surprised her.

Cleo frowned. 'You do know it's way up in North Queensland?'

'That's all right. I have my own plane. The site will have a runway, surely.'

'Well, no, it doesn't. It's served by road and railway. You'll have to land at Townsville and drive the rest of the way. It's about thirty kilometres.'

'No trouble. I'll have Grace organise a suitable vehicle to meet us at Townsville airport.'

Cleo blinked. *'Us?'*

'Yes, you're coming with me.'

CHAPTER FIVE

BYRON ENJOYED THE shock on her face, almost as much as he'd enjoyed her loosening up over the course of the meal.

Now, suddenly, she was looking very worried.

'Is there a problem with your coming with me?' he asked. 'Would your husband object?'

'What?' Her eyes flew to her left hand where she twisted the gold band on her left finger for a second or two before looking up again. 'No. Martin won't object,' she said with a somewhat sad sigh. 'He can't. He…he died some time ago.'

Shock—and something else—had Byron sitting up straight in his chair. So she was a widow. Not unhappily married, or divorced. Just a lady with a sad past and likely *way* too much emotional baggage.

Byron knew he should steer well clear. He didn't need to deviate from the path he'd set himself. Which was finding the right girl to marry. Clearly, Cleo wasn't that girl.

But despite all that he was finding her perversely attractive. Even more than he had back at his office. As she'd let down her defences, he'd seen more evidence that she found him as attractive as he found her. The way her eyes had sparkled at him every now and then. Quite lovely eyes, they were. The loveliest feature she had. Though her mouth was very kissable too. You just didn't focus on it without lipstick. He couldn't really see her figure underneath that ghastly pant suit, but she wasn't overweight. He suspected there was a nice curvy shape under there somewhere. Byron liked curves.

It was a truly weird situation, one fraught with danger. He should not be thinking about having sex with her. A wise man did not mix business with pleasure. But he was thinking just that. Oh, yes, he definitely was.

'How long ago?' he asked, hiding his lustful thoughts behind a quiet voice.

'Just over three years.'

A long time for her to be without a man. And it was obvious by the way she'd presented herself today that she hadn't been out there, dating again. Cleo had the look of a woman still in mourning, a woman who'd forgotten what it was like to be a woman.

Until today, that was…

Byron sensed that something had changed for Cleo today. His male ego suggested it was he who'd changed her. He knew he was attractive to women, having been blessed with the kind of face and body women fancied. Even when girls didn't know he was filthy rich, they came onto him. Byron didn't think Cleo was interested in his money. He doubted she was seriously interested in him at all. Otherwise, she'd jump at the chance of being alone with him.

No. If he wanted this woman—and he did, by God!—he would have to seduce her. She wasn't about to make it easy for him.

The prospect both challenged and aroused Byron. How long had it been since he'd actually had to seduce a woman? Five years? Ten? *Twenty?* In truth, he'd *never* had to.

His flesh stirred further at how satisfying it was going to be, once he succeeded. Satisfying for her as well as him. He was a good lover. And a confident one. She wouldn't regret going to bed with him.

'You're very young to be a widow, Cleo,' he said. 'If you don't mind me asking, how did your husband die?'

'Cancer. A very malignant melanoma, which wouldn't quit, no matter what the doctors threw at it. Martin fought it with every ounce of his being. But it was too strong for him in the end,' she finished up, her eyes moistening at the memory.

A momentary guilt threatened to derail Byron's lust. But she couldn't grieve for her husband for ever, no matter how much she'd loved him or how tragic his demise. Life moved on. She had to move on. And he was just the man to help her do so.

Byron's conscience decided magnanimously that his taking Cleo to bed would be the best thing for her. She needed someone to bring her back to life, and he was just the man to do it!

'That's very sad, Cleo,' he said gently. 'Cancer is the very devil, isn't it? My mother had breast cancer a few years ago, but thankfully she survived.'

'Then she's very lucky.'

'Indeed. She's going to turn sixty next weekend. She's having a big bash of a party,' he went on, reminding himself that he would have to attend. She was sure to have lined up a prospective daughter-in-law or two for him to look over, Byron having been foolish enough to confide in his mother recently that he really did want to get married and give her grandchildren.

'Perhaps you'd like to come with me?' he said impulsively, despite knowing the invitation was both presumptuous and premature.

Cleo stared at him as though he'd just asked her to accompany him to the moon.

'You want me to go to your mother's birthday party with you?' she asked him incredulously.

'Yes. Why not?' He wasn't about to back-pedal. Byron never back-pedalled.

'I think *why* is more like the right question,' she countered brusquely.

'Do I need a reason?'

'Yes.'

'Because I like you and find your company stimulating.'

Her smile was wry. 'Now what's the real reason?'

He could hardly tell her that it had been an impulse invitation, one driven by his darker side. But now that he'd made it, he could see that it actually had potential in a more practical sense.

'You've forced it out of me,' he said, smiling back just as wryly. 'The thing is, my dearest mother is keen for me to settle down and have a family, so there's bound to be a few potential brides for my perusal at this event.

Since I would prefer to pick my own future wife, I need protection from her matchmaking. If I show up with a woman of my own choice on my arm, I might have a chance of actually enjoying myself.'

Cleo couldn't help it. She laughed.

'As much as I would like to help you out,' she said, still chuckling inside, 'I'm afraid I'll have to say no.'

'Why?' he asked, sounding most put out. Clearly, not many women said no to Byron.

Cleo listed all the reasons in her head.

Because I don't have a thing to wear to such an occasion.

Because I would be like a fish out of water in your mother's social circle.

Because none of the guests would believe I was really your date.

Because I don't want to torture myself by pretending to be your date.

'Because I don't actually enjoy parties,' she said instead. 'Sorry. I'm sure you can find someone else to be your pretend girlfriend for one night.'

'Actually no, I can't,' he growled as he pulled a face. 'I'm between fiancées at the moment.'

Cleo smiled ruefully. 'How unfortunate,' she murmured, amused by his little-boy pout. 'Still, I would imagine you know scores of unattached women who would jump at the chance of accompanying you.'

'True. But all of them would also jump to the conclusion that they were in with a chance to become fiancée number three.'

Cleo bristled at the implication that *she* wouldn't do any such thing. And she knew why. Because she was far too ordinary to contemplate anything so extraordinary. The woman who eventually wore Byron's wedding ring on her finger would be out of the ordinary in every way. He wasn't about to settle for just anyone. He'd already discarded a Victoria's Secret model and a stunning actress. Cleo momentarily wondered what it was about them that had caused those break-ups. The articles she'd read about Byron suggested the splits had been *his* doing. But who knew? Maybe he was a player, even when he was engaged. Wealthy men often were.

'Come on, Cleo,' he said with a very bewitching smile. 'Help me out here.'

It annoyed Cleo how tempted she was to say yes, an answer she knew she would instantly regret. As fascinating as she found Byron, no way would she put herself in a position that would ultimately be humiliating. Neither did she like the idea of being used. It also worried her that this attraction she was feeling could escalate into infatuation, if she spent too much time with him. And she didn't want that. In truth, Cleo rather liked her independent existence. It made for a stress-free personal life, leaving her to concentrate on the one thing she genuinely enjoyed and that she could count on: her job. The last thing she needed were the emotional upsets that inevitably came with relationships. Just look at the mess Sarah and Scott had been in this past week or so. Far better to steer well clear of the opposite sex, even if it meant spending the rest of her life alone.

Of course, she hadn't counted on her libido coming

back to life in such a remarkable fashion. Still, it was nothing that wouldn't simmer down, in time. It was a pity she had to spend tomorrow with him. But she was certain she could remain professional in his presence, especially if she established proper boundaries now.

'I'm sorry, Byron,' she told him coolly. 'But I really can't. Maybe you should just go to your mother's party alone and face the music.'

'You don't know my mother,' he said drily.

'Perhaps you should just tell her that you don't want to get married; that you prefer the life of a…a bachelor.' She'd almost said playboy, but had known instinctively that he wouldn't like that tag. Admittedly, Byron wasn't known for being a heartless womaniser, but his two broken engagements had had a lot of publicity.

A heavy sigh wafted from Byron's lungs, his eyes rolling in exasperation. 'That's the crux of the problem. The fact is, I *do* want to get married. But only to the right sort of girl, not the kind my mother would dish up to me.'

'I see,' Cleo said slowly. 'And what kind is that?'

'Oh, you know,' he said, waving his hand around in a circular fashion. 'Society princesses whose only aim in life is to marry well, which translates to a husband with money. And lots of it. Then they can live in a Double Bay mansion, dress in designer clothes and have their children looked after by nannies whilst they sit on charity boards or do ladies' luncheons in between holidays to Tuscany, or possibly to New York, where they can shop their greedy little hearts out.'

Cleo was taken aback by his cynical tirade.

'You don't *have* to marry any of them,' she pointed out.

'I don't intend to,' he said ruefully. 'Now. Do you want coffee? Or would you prefer a cognac?'

CHAPTER SIX

CLEO RANG SCOTT when she got back to the office, still slightly tipsy, at three-thirty. The time difference between Sydney and Thailand was three hours so she figured Scott would have to be awake. He answered after a few rings, sounding happy.

'So how did it go with Maddox?' he asked.

Cleo cut straight to the chase. 'He wants to visit the refinery. Tomorrow,' she added. 'In his private jet.'

'Oh, hell. That could be a disaster.'

Cleo agreed, but not for the reasons Scott was talking about. Already she was looking forward to seeing Byron again.

'He has to know the truth sooner or later,' she said with her usual pragmatism.

Scott sighed. 'Tell him I'm planning on closing it down until the nickel prices go back up again.'

'That might be wise.'

'Aside from that, what did you think of the man?'

'Not sure yet. He's very suave. And way too sure of himself.'

'That's what Sarah said. She wasn't a fan when we met him at the races last year. But possibly that was because she didn't like his fiancée. I gather she's no longer in the picture, but, still, the crucial point is…does he have shifty eyes?'

Cleo wasn't sure what he was talking about for a second, until she recalled how she'd recently dismissed a potential investor because he had shifty eyes.

'No,' she said with a dry laugh. Byron's eyes weren't at all shifty. Instead they were very blue and very beautiful, fringed by lashes that any woman would envy. They were also knowing and intelligent and sexy as hell.

'Good,' Scott said. 'So you liked him, then? In the business sense, that is?'

'I suppose so. I'll be able to make a better judgment after tomorrow. Do you want me to ring you again tomorrow night, after I get back?'

Scott's hesitation was telling. 'No,' he said at last. 'No, don't do that. I promised Sarah to put work aside for these next two weeks and that's what I intend doing. Not much I can do from here, anyway. I trust you to make the right calls, Cleo. Only ring me from now on if there's an emergency.'

'Okay.' She decided not to mention that Byron's accountant was coming to check the books tomorrow as well. He and Sarah obviously needed this time together without the distraction of the business. It wasn't as though there was anything to worry about. Their own accountant was both meticulous and ethical. Scott didn't hire any other kind of employee, though he always did a full background check before he employed anyone.

Cleo decided it might be wise to do one on Byron Maddox. Looking up articles on the Internet didn't quite match a full security check. As soon as she got off the phone to Scott, Cleo rang Harvey, their head of security.

'Harvey,' she said. 'I have a rush job for you.'

'Shoot.' Harvey was a man of few words.

'I want you to find out everything you can for me on Byron Maddox.' Cleo refused to concede that there was a measure of feminine curiosity driving her request. This was strictly business. Scott was trusting her to negotiate with this man and she wasn't going to let him down. People always said knowledge was power. That was what Cleo felt she needed before tomorrow. More power.

'*The* Byron Maddox?' Harvey said, sounding surprised.

'Yes. I have an important business meeting with him tomorrow. Could you email me a full report by ten tonight?'

'Will do. *Boss*,' he added on a drily humorous note, then hung up.

Cleo was smiling as she hung up. She'd rather liked being called boss. What a shame she didn't have millions of dollars. Then she could have put herself forward as Scott's new partner, instead of trying to con Byron Maddox into taking the job.

And it would be a con. Because no businessman in his right mind was going to invest in the mining industry at the moment. The only way to make it palatable would be for Scott to offer a fifty per cent partnership in McAllister Mines at a very reduced price. Which he just might be prepared to do. *When* he got back. Meanwhile, it was up to Cleo to keep Byron sweet.

The thought came that maybe she *should* have accepted his ridiculous invitation to go to his mother's birthday party. Obviously, Byron didn't realise she would be an embarrassment to him. Possibly he imagined that she was one of those women who after work could transform herself into a *femme fatale*. Cleo had seen a perfume ad on TV once where the prissy secretary suddenly whipped down her hair, shrugged out of her jacket, slapped on some red lipstick, undid the top buttons of her silky blouse, and—*whammo*! Instant vamp!

Cleo knew she wasn't capable of achieving that kind of miracle, even if she spent hours on herself. She'd never had any fashion sense, or know-how when it came to hairstyles and make-up. It would be easy to blame her grandmother's influence for her lack of style. And there was no doubt her grandmother's old-fashioned ways were a contributing factor. But Cleo suspected it was something she'd been born with. Some people—like Scott's wife, Sarah—had an innate sense of style. They knew exactly what suited them and how to make the best of themselves. Cleo had never had that ability. She'd been a shy teenager, lacking confidence in her looks. She'd always thought herself plain, with a too big mouth and too big everything. Breasts. Bum. Thighs. No wonder she'd still been a virgin when she'd met Martin at university. And no wonder she'd been bowled over when he'd said how pretty he thought she was, and how much he liked the way she dressed, complimenting her on wearing no make-up and not looking like a tart.

In hindsight, she understood full well that Martin had liked her not looking too good, especially after her puppy fat had melted away and her figure had improved dramatically. But by then the damage to her self-esteem had been done, and she'd got into the habit of dressing like a dowdy spinster, consoling herself with the fact that Martin loved her for herself. Even after they were married and she'd realised that her husband's compliments about her modest clothes were his way of controlling her, Cleo had seemed incapable of doing herself up differently. After Martin had become ill, she'd no longer cared what she looked like. It was only when she'd become Scott's PA that she'd made a conscious effort to at least smarten up her working wardrobe.

Not altogether successfully, she feared. Seeing Byron's PA today had come as a bit of a shock. She envied how Grace looked, wishing she could look half as good. If she did, she would have accepted Byron's invitation like a shot. She might even have stood a slim chance of having her erotic fantasies about him fulfilled.

This last thought made her laugh. Men like Byron Maddox didn't sleep with ordinary girls like Cleo. They bedded supermodels, and drop-dead gorgeous actresses. Cleo wouldn't mind betting that he was already relieved that she'd said no to accompanying him to his mother's birthday. To imagine that he might ask her again was pure fantasy.

Sighing with a mixture of disappointment and resignation, Cleo lifted her phone to call their accountant before he left to go home. She had to warn him that Byron's accountant would be dropping by to check the books. He sounded somewhat peeved but that was just too bad. She wasn't exactly thrilled at having to fly to Townsville at some ungodly hour the next morning, either.

Tomorrow stretched in front of Cleo as one long trial. It wasn't going to be easy keeping her business head on in the presence of a man who did dreadful things to her hormones without even trying. She was about to close down her computer and head for Central station when her phone rang.

Cleo's eyebrows went ceilingwards at the identity of her caller.

'Hello, Byron,' she answered crisply. 'Is there a problem with tomorrow's arrangements?'

'Do you always assume that there's a problem when a man calls you?'

'That depends on the man,' she said, shocked that her voice was decidedly flirty. She *never* did flirty.

Until now.

Damn the man!

Down the line, Byron wasn't sure what to think. Maybe Cleo wasn't as sexually repressed as he'd imagined.

Good, he decided.

'Sounds like you've had some difficult men in your life,' he said. 'Look, I was thinking that maybe we should stay overnight in Townsville. Otherwise, it's going to be a very long day. I'll get Grace to make a hotel booking for us. Is that all right with you?'

Byron wasn't planning any major seduction—not in Townsville anyway. He just wanted some more time to get to know her. Cleo Shelton was a rather intriguing woman.

'I don't see a problem with that,' she stated, an underlying hint of reserve in her reply.

'Fine. I'll still pick you up at your house at seven. We

should be in the air by eight-thirty at the latest. Bring something to wear to dinner,' he suggested, wanting to see her in a dress.

'People don't get dressed up in Townsville, Byron,' she said somewhat brusquely.

'Fine. I'll just bring a change of jeans then. And a fresh shirt.'

'Sounds perfect. I'll do the same.'

He pictured her in tight jeans and thought, yes, that would do. For starters.

'Great. See you in the morning, then.'

'I'll be ready,' she said before terminating the call at her end.

Byron had no doubt she would be. Grace had said she wasn't the type of girl to be late. And he knew why. It was because she didn't spend hours on her hair and face. The women Byron usually dated were always running late, due to their endless titivating.

Of course, tomorrow wasn't a date. It was a business appointment. He had to keep telling himself that. When Cleo finally agreed to go to his mother's party with him—he aimed to ask her again—he wouldn't be surprised to discover a different creature. Women constantly surprised him over how different they could look in different clothes, and with a different hairstyle.

If *she comes with you,* a small voice intruded all of a sudden, one which didn't bob up in his head too often. It was the same voice that had appeared shortly after his father left his mother, when Byron had been just sixteen. A very vulnerable age. It was the voice of insecurity, one which reminded him that, sometimes, life served you up something you couldn't have, or win. Byron had grown up thinking he could have—or win—whatever he wanted. His father leaving his mother had rocked his world. For several months, father and son had been bitterly estranged, until his mother had confessed that *she* had been the cause of the divorce, that she'd had an affair and that his sister, Lara, was not Lloyd's biological daughter.

Of course, she still blamed her husband.

'He was always away on business,' she'd wailed at the time. 'I was lonely.'

As if that excused adultery!

She'd only confessed to her son because her husband had made a deal with her.

'Clear things with Byron and I'll accept Lara as my daughter.'

Lara didn't know she wasn't Lloyd Maddox's biological daughter and Byron was once again close to the man he'd always admired. They were still close, despite the massive falling-out they'd had five years ago about some financial advice Byron had given his father that hadn't been taken. Lloyd had listened instead to some sycophantic idiot whom Byron couldn't stand. As a consequence, Byron had severed all professional ties with his father and come home to start his own business, concentrating on quality investments rather than quantity.

But he wasn't a man who held grudges and had made up with his father ages ago. His father was his best friend and his confidant. Lloyd knew his son wanted to marry and have a family, and had advised him just last week not to settle for anything less than the right kind of wife.

'Nothing like your mother for starters,' he'd warned him. 'We Maddox men need independent partners with careers of their own, otherwise we'll end up treating them badly. I treated your mother badly because she didn't stand up to me. She just said yes, dear, no, dear, and three bags full, dear. That kind of subservient attitude doesn't engender respect. I have to admit I never admired her more than when she actually cheated on me. I deserved it. Truly.'

Byron had been taken aback at this confession. Lloyd was not one to take the blame for anything. In truth, he was an arrogant man, always expecting things to go his way.

A bit like you, Byron, came another voice that occasionally troubled him. His conscience, he supposed. He did have one. Though he didn't always listen to it.

This last train of thought brought him back to a certain lady whom he knew he really shouldn't pursue. As he'd told himself earlier today, he should be out there looking for a wife, not thinking about having an affair with Cleo Shelton. Which was all it would be. An affair. He didn't need the emotional baggage a young widow would carry with her. Those damned male hormones of his were leading him astray again.

Even if Cleo *was* wife material, she herself wasn't on the lookout for another husband. He knew how such women acted when that was their agenda and it wasn't even remotely on Cleo's radar. Cleo's sadness when talking about her dead husband suggested that she mourned him still, and that wasn't something Byron wanted to become involved in.

But that didn't mean she couldn't ever have sex again, Byron decided, swiftly putting aside his misgivings about having an affair with Cleo, embracing the idea with his usual decisiveness and positivity. Finding a wife could wait. It was, after all, only six weeks since he'd split with Simone. He really needed more time to recover from the disappointment of having been wrong once again. He hesitated to use the word *devastated*. Byron was no hypocrite. But it had hurt. It really had.

Meanwhile, he would seek comfort for his bruised ego with an intriguing brunette who he suspected was hiding a secretly sensual nature. She'd flirted with him on the phone just now. Oh, yes, she definitely had.

With his conscience firmly routed and his testosterone firing, Byron stood up and walked out to tell Grace to make a booking for them at a hotel in Townsville.

'So you and Cleo are having a sleepover,' she said with a rather knowing look.

'Very funny, Grace. Just make the booking, will you?'

'Motel or hotel?'

'Either. Just make sure it has a good restaurant. We'll be too tired to go out.'

'What did Cleo say about this?' Grace asked as she tapped away on her computer.

'She didn't sound too thrilled,' came his honest reply. 'But what could she say but yes? If she wants me to invest in McAllister Mines, then she has to play ball.'

Grace gave him a closed look. 'Something tells me that Cleo is not the kind of girl who will play that sort of game.'

'I don't know what you mean, Grace.'

'You know very well what I mean, Byron. She's not what you're used to.'

'And what am I used to?'

'May I be honest here without risking my job?'

'Of course.' He'd always encouraged Grace to give him honest opinions. His father might like sycophantic assistants, but Byron did not.

'In that case let me say that you've grown used to women who do whatever you want them to do. Unfortunately, most of them have a gold wedding band in their eyes when they suck up to you and tell you how wonderful you are. Your two ex-fiancées might have been stunning to look at but underneath their surface beauty lay the most shallow, selfish, cold-blooded creatures I have ever met.'

'I do know that, Grace,' Byron countered, shocked by Grace's cripplingly accurate observations. 'And your point is?'

'Cleo Shelton is none of those things. She's a *nice* girl.'

'And how, pray tell, do you know that? You've known her all of five minutes.'

'I just do. Call it feminine intuition,' she added with a touch of asperity. 'I would hate to see you toy with her emotions. You're an exceedingly attractive man, Byron. Even without your money you would turn any woman's head.'

'I know of one woman in my life whose head isn't turned,' he said crossly as he glared at her.

'Yes, well, I'm happily married. And I've been around enough rich men in my life to know they are not for me, no matter how handsome and charming they are.'

Byron winced under words that were not compliments. Grace made handsome and charming sound like serious flaws.

'I noticed the wedding ring on Cleo's left hand,' she went on before Byron could speak, or leave. 'I hope you did, too.'

Byron was glad to have the final word. 'I certainly did,' he replied, trying not to sound smug. 'But you don't have to worry that your dastardly boss is about to toy with a married woman's emotions. Cleo is a widow.' And without further explanation, he marched back into his office, closing the door firmly behind him.

CHAPTER SEVEN

'YOU WON'T BE needing that,' were Byron's first words when Cleo answered her door at seven the following morning. He nodded down at the overnight bag that was sitting by the front door. 'I realised late last night that I have to be back here in Sydney for an important business meeting on Friday morning. Sorry. I would have rung you only I thought you might not be up.'

Cleo wasn't sure if she was relieved or disappointed. One part of her was slightly annoyed at all the time she'd taken deciding what to bring to wear to dinner tonight. Her options had been minimal. She did own a couple of dresses but both were dated, and on the dreary side. In the end, she'd packed her newest navy pant suit and borrowed a pale pink blouse from Doreen's wardrobe. Not ideal, but better than the dresses.

Doreen had asked her a few questions about Byron, with Cleo dismissing him as typical of bachelor billionaires.

'You know the type,' she'd said off-handedly. 'They think they're irresistible to women.'

The trouble was...they *were*. Or Byron was. He'd been

handsome enough yesterday in his sleek grey suit. But in faded blue jeans, a white polo shirt and a black leather bomber jacket he was drop-dead gorgeous. And sinfully sexy. Cleo was glad Doreen was still asleep in bed and not peering out of her bedroom window at him.

'Okay,' she said. 'Just have to get my handbag.'

She picked up her smartphone, which contained the all-important report from Harvey that had arrived last night but which Cleo had only skimmed through so far. There were no real surprises that she could see, but she planned on having a more thorough perusal during the plane trip up to Townsville, especially the long list of the investments the BM Group had made these past five years. They were many and varied, she'd noted, but none were in the mining industry.

Cleo suspected she was wasting her time today. Byron would not bail Scott out. Especially after he'd spoken to the manager of the refinery. Still, she had to try, didn't she? And if she were strictly honest with herself, she *wanted* to spend the day in Byron's stimulating company; wanted to accompany him on his private jet and luxuriate in a world over which she could only fantasise.

'Ready to go now?' Byron said rather abruptly when she returned to the front door with her handbag. Only then did she notice that he looked tired, with some dark shadows under his eyes. A late night, she speculated, as she followed him out into the street.

The thought of his being up until the wee hours of the night with some nameless but undoubtedly beautiful creature did not sit well with Cleo. Which was ridiculous.

The man was free to do exactly as he pleased, since he was between fiancées at the moment.

As reasonable as this logic was, it still caused the appearance of a dark and decidedly unpleasant sensation that Cleo had never experienced before. She felt fairly certain that it was jealousy. Or was it envy? Yes, that was what it was. Envy.

'Come along, then,' he said. 'Lock the door and let's get going.'

Cleo smothered a sigh, and got going.

'I wasn't able to find a parking space,' Byron told her as he led Cleo out to his double-parked Lexus.

'There's an alleyway around the back which usually has plenty of spots,' she informed him. 'But no matter. You don't seem to have held anybody up.'

'True.' Not a soul was stirring in the street, except for one old chap walking his dog.

Byron opened the passenger door for Cleo, shaking his head as he watched her climb in, puzzled over why he found this woman so damned attractive. Her looks weren't anything to write home about, and she made absolutely no effort at all with her appearance. Take what she was wearing today. Dark blue jeans, which were neither well fitted nor slimming, teamed with another white shirt and what looked like the same hideous black jacket she'd worn yesterday. Still no make-up or perfume, or anything that smacked of femininity. As for her hair... His fingers literally itched to pull apart that awful bun thing, which seemed permanently anchored at the nape of her neck.

It was actually very nice hair, he conceded. Dark and thick and shiny. And with a natural wave in it. He could see a few kinks, despite its severely scraped-back style. It would look much better down around her face and spread out over her shoulders.

Or over a pillow, came the gut-crunching thought.

Gritting his teeth, Byron slammed the door and marched around to the other side, angry with himself for not being able to control his thoughts—and his carnal desires—around this woman. Yet he was determined to.

After leaving work yesterday and riding the lift up to his penthouse, he hadn't been able to get Grace's disparaging comment about his toying with Cleo's emotions out of his mind. Byron knew he wasn't a bad man. Spoiled, possibly. And used to getting his own way. But not at the expense of others, he hoped.

To seduce Cleo—*and, let's face it, Byron, that's what it would end up being*—would not be very gallant of him. And he clearly wouldn't be doing it for *her* benefit, as he'd previously managed to convince himself. It would be all about satisfying his own desire.

Thank God he'd remembered his golf game with Blake on Friday. It gave him a legitimate excuse to cancel the stopover and fly straight back after the visit to the refinery. When he couldn't sleep last night, Byron had done some further research on McAllister Mines, focusing on the nickel refinery. He wasn't surprised to find that it was a dead loss. Nickel prices had crashed and didn't look like recovering for years. McAllister should have closed it down ages ago. The man was either a fool or too generous for his own good. He almost rang Cleo and cancelled the visit altogether, but he just couldn't do it.

Byron told himself it was because he could see how much it meant to her to try to convince him to invest in McAllister Mines. He told himself that it would be cruel not to give her one last chance to sell him on the idea of being McAllister's business partner.

He'd lied to himself. The truth was, he'd just wanted to see her again, despite his firm resolve not to pursue her. Talk about masochism!

'So what was the important business meeting you'd forgotten?' she asked him once he'd executed a three-point turn and headed for the airport.

Byron sighed. 'I have to play golf.'

'Golf,' she echoed, disbelief in her voice.

'I know what you're thinking. A game of golf hardly sounds like a proper business meeting. But trust me when I say it is. I actually loathe the game. It drives me nuts!' Only because he wasn't good at it.

'Then why play it?'

'Because Blake Randall likes to do business over a game of golf.'

'And who's Blake Randall?'

'He's the head of Fantasy Productions. They make movies. Have you see *The Boy from the Bush*?'

'Oh, yes, I have. I loved it.'

'That's one of his. Blake directed that one. But he's moved on from directing these days. He's more into production, and Hollywood is calling. Big time.'

'Am I right in presuming you want to invest in his company?'

'You are.'

'I would imagine that movies are even riskier than mining,' Cleo pointed out.

'Depends on who's at the helm. Blake has a record second to none. He's a bloody genius.'

'Takes one to know one, I guess,' she said just as he stopped at a set of lights.

Her compliment startled Byron. His head turned to look at her. 'Flattery, Cleo? Something tells me that's not like you.'

She blushed. She actually blushed. The pink brought a glow to her face, and a touching vulnerability to her usually cool eyes. He ached to bend over and kiss her, to see if she would come alive even further under his mouth.

But before he could give in to temptation, the lights turned green.

'It's not. Usually,' she said in rather droll tones. 'But I'm a desperate woman. I would hate for Scott to think I didn't throw everything at you to get you on side. He really needs a new partner, Byron, and, as you can imagine, investors are not exactly lining up to get on board.'

Interesting, he thought. He liked that she was desperate. Liked that she would do just about anything to get him on board.

Don't do this, Byron, his conscience insisted. *Don't take advantage of the situation.*

'In that case,' he said, ignoring the voice in his head, 'how about reconsidering my invitation to accompany me to my mother's birthday party on Saturday night? Not only will you help me out enormously,' he went on before she could protest, 'but by then, I'll have the report from my accountant and I'll be able to give you a definite decision on whether I will invest in McAllister Mines or not.'

Her groan carried frustration. 'Look, I'd honestly like to go with you. But I can't.'

'Why's that?'

'Oh, for heaven's sake, don't be so obtuse,' she snapped. 'Your mother would take one look at me and think you'd gone mad. No one would believe for a second that I was your date for real.'

'Why not?'

Her sigh was heavy. 'You know why not. If the fashion police could arrest people, I'd be in jail right now.'

Byron refused to be swayed. 'Don't be ridiculous. You're a very attractive woman. With the right dress, hairstyle and make-up, you would be a stunner.'

'That's the problem. I don't have the right dress. And I haven't a clue about hairstyles or make-up.'

Byron finally got past his own selfish wishes to consider what she was saying. 'But why is that, Cleo?' he asked. 'I mean, most girls these days are clued up on such things from the earliest ages. Take my kid sister, Lara. She's been experimenting with make-up since she was ten, much to my mother's disgust. Same with hairstyles, and hair colour. Her latest is blue, would you believe? As for clothes, Lara's favourite occupation is shopping for the latest gear.'

'How old is your sister?' Cleo asked.

'Nineteen.'

'Well, I'm *twenty*-nine, Byron.'

And you dress like you're fifty-nine, he thought.

'That makes you six years younger than me, madam. You're a young woman, Cleo, so stop with the excuses and explain why you haven't a clue about all things female. Come on. *Give.*'

She rolled her eyes at him. 'Did anyone ever tell you that you're bossy?'

He shrugged. 'Not that I recall.'

She laughed. 'Possibly because they wouldn't dare. Okay, if you must know, I was an only child, and shy. My parents were killed in a car accident when I was thirteen, and I was raised by my elderly and very old-fashioned grandparents. My grandmother was dead against make-up and immodest clothes as well as going against Mother Nature. And my husband *liked* the way I looked, so I never saw any reason to change.'

'Do *you* like the way you look, Cleo?' he asked, thinking to himself that he didn't much like the sound of her husband.

Her chin lifted but her eyes carried uncertainty. 'I know I could look better. But like I said earlier,' she added with a frustrated sigh, 'I just don't know what to do.'

'Then get someone to help you,' he advised, a little impatiently. 'There are professional stylists who will sort out your wardrobe. And any decent beauty salon will know how to do your hair and make-up. You just have to decide to do it, Cleo.'

'But what would be the point?' she said, sounding annoyingly defeatist.

'The point would be that when a man asks you out, you will happily go! Or do you want to spend the rest of your life without a social life?' *Or a sex life,* he thought but didn't say. 'Look, Grace will know who to put you in touch with. I'll get her to contact you tomorrow. Now no more objections,' he said when she opened her mouth to protest. 'You are going to the party with me and that's that!'

CHAPTER EIGHT

CLEO KNEW SHE should continue to protest. The man was like a bulldozer, running roughshod over her feelings. And her life. Normally, she wouldn't stand for such behaviour. But somehow Byron didn't offend her the way another man would have. So instead of opening her mouth and making some futile objection—and it would be futile, she knew—Cleo settled back in the superbly comfortable leather seat, doing her best to look coolly resigned, instead of secretly excited. Because she did want to go with him, didn't she? The only thing stopping her was fear over making a fool of herself.

'I'll contact Grace from the plane,' Byron said. 'She won't be in the office yet and I don't like to ring her at home.'

'Why's that?' Cleo asked, proud of her composed demeanour. 'Scott often rings me at home.' Her boss had made it clear from day one that being his PA would not be a nine-to-five job.

'That's because you don't have a husband to object. Oh, I'm so sorry. That was insensitive of me.'

'No, don't apologise,' she replied a little stiffly. The

last thing she wanted to think about at that moment was Martin. 'Frankly, I'm glad I don't have a husband at home to object.' And Martin would have, no doubt about that. Not that she would have ever had her present job if Martin had been alive and well. She would not have even been working at McAllister Mines if that had been the case—she would have left Martin *and* her job. Lord knew where she would be by now, if that had happened. Certainly not here, in this gorgeous car, sitting beside a gorgeous though slightly irritating man.

'You don't want to get married again, Cleo?'

An involuntary shudder ran through her before she could stop it. 'No,' she said with faked calm. 'No, I don't.' She didn't have to explain why to him. She imagined lots of widows didn't want to get married again. Doreen never had, for the same reason Cleo didn't. Madly controlling husbands left behind women who were wary of trusting their lives to a man ever again.

'What about children?' he asked.

Cleo's heart twisted. She had wanted children. At first. But even that desire had been ripped out of her once she'd recognised the hell her life would be as a stay-at-home mother with Martin at the helm and his children having to follow endless rules and restrictions.

'I did want children,' she confessed. 'But Martin insisted on paying our mortgage off first so that I could leave work when I fell pregnant. But before that happened, he was diagnosed with cancer. Since I don't want to get married again, children are out of the question.'

'Not really. You don't have to be married to have a baby.'

Such a thought had never crossed Cleo's mind. But now that it did, she didn't like it much. 'I don't want to be a single mother.'

'Fair enough. Ah, here we are.'

Cleo was glad that *that* conversation had been terminated. Hopefully, Byron wouldn't bring up the subject of marriage and children ever again. She did her best not to gasp at the sight of the fabulous-looking jet that stood waiting for them on the tarmac. It wasn't enormous. But it was the stuff dreams were made of. White and glistening in the morning sun, it had sleekly powerful lines that promised speed and the total luxury of private plane travel.

'Yes, it's quite something, isn't it?' Byron said as he helped her out of the car then led her up the steps, which actually had a red carpet running up the middle. 'It's a Gulfstream. It can accommodate twelve passengers and can fly over seven thousand miles non-stop.'

'Goodness.'

Cleo tried not to gape, or gawk, as she was led through the open doorway into the jet's interior. Talk about utter luxury! There were heaps of cream leather seats, some arranged around rich walnut tables. After that there was a home theatre and a beautifully equipped kitchen, opposite which was an unbelievably spacious bathroom. Beyond that Cleo glimpsed a bedroom, which had a door that could obviously close for complete privacy.

'This must have cost you a small fortune,' she blurted out before she could think better of it.

'Not a single cent,' he told her. 'It belongs to my father. He's here in Australia at the moment. He said I could use it, so I am. It's rather over the top, isn't it?'

'Oh, no, I think it's fabulous!' she said, finally giving in to the urge to gush.

He smiled. 'Pleased you like it. Now, best sit down and buckle up. I can feel we're already on the move.'

All the seats on the left side were window seats. After Cleo chose one, Byron sat down in the seat directly across the aisle from her.

'I'm afraid there's no steward to serve us drinks or anything,' he told her. 'Once we're airborne, I'll raid the kitchen for some food and drinks. I haven't eaten anything yet.'

'That's very naughty of you,' she said. 'Breakfast is the most important meal of the day.'

'Then I must be a very naughty boy. Because I rarely have breakfast. Of course, I do usually stay up late. And I have dinner late.'

Cleo didn't want to think about the reasons for him always staying up late.

Her eyes slid across the aisle, surreptitiously looking him over. His profile was striking and she could hardly tear her eyes from his face. She was going to a party with him this Saturday night.

Her stomach fizzed at the thought.

'Don't forget to contact Grace once she's in the office,' she reminded him. Now that she'd agreed to go to that party with Byron, she wanted to look as good as she possibly could. The thought of embracing a substantial makeover was daunting. But she was determined.

His head turned her way, his smile wry. 'I won't forget.'

Just then the plane accelerated down the runway and took off, Cleo gripping the arm rests as it did so. She wasn't afraid of flying, but she didn't like take-offs. As a distraction, she gazed down at the view below, thinking what a beautiful city Sydney was. Before long, however, the jet headed out to sea then up into the air and there was nothing to see but clouds. The seat-belt sign was switched off and Byron stood up straight away.

'Time,' he said, 'for some refreshments.'

He returned with a bottle of champagne and two glasses.

'Surely that's not all you're having,' she chided as he poured.

'What are you,' he said, 'the food police?'

'Very funny.'

'A first-class flight always starts with a glass of champagne. And don't tell me you don't like champagne because I won't believe you.'

'I do like champagne.'

'Good. Then drink up.'

It was utterly delicious and no doubt as expensive as everything else around her.

Byron settled back down and took a long swallow, a thoughtful expression on his face. Finally, he turned to glance over at her.

'If you were me, would you invest in McAllister Mines?'

Cleo's smile carried dry amusement. 'Now that's not fair, Byron, and you know it.'

'Business dealings are rarely fair, Cleo.'

'They *can* be,' she contradicted. 'Scott is always fair in his business dealings.'

'Which is perhaps why he's in financial difficulties. You have to be ruthless to survive in business these days, Cleo.'

This rather harsh opinion brought a stab of disappointment. Still, she should have known he'd be as ruthless as his father. This thought reminded Cleo that she needed to have a more thorough look through Harvey's report. It would be naive of her to take everything Byron said at face value. As bewitchingly attractive and charming as he was, he was still Lloyd Maddox's son.

Putting down her near empty champagne glass in the drink holder next to her, Cleo bent to extract her phone from her handbag, which she'd dropped at her feet.

'Would you mind terribly if I did some work for a while? I need to check my emails, plus I have a few to send myself.' Total lies. But you had to be ruthless in business, didn't you?

'Go right ahead. I'm going to catch up on some shut-eye.'

Harvey's report didn't really tell her all that much more than she'd already gleaned herself via the Internet. There were some additional but rather dry details about his birth, his background and very privileged upbringing. He'd been born in a private clinic in Sydney thirty-five years ago. He'd been an only child until his mother had a girl, sixteen years later. Lara Audrey. Byron's middle name was Augustus, the same as his grandfather, who'd been a newspaper proprietor in Sydney in the fifties. He'd been educated at the exclusive River-view College, was dux of his school, as well as captain of various sports teams and the debating team.

Which meant he would be a good negotiator. Or liar. Or both.

After graduating school, he'd had a gap year travelling Europe and the Americas, ending with Christmas spent with his father in New York. His parents had been divorced a while by then. Amicably, it seemed. After returning home, the nineteen-year-old Byron started a business degree at Sydney University, barely scraping through during his first year but then knuckling down and gaining distinctions in all his subjects from then on. Not high distinctions, she noted ruefully, perhaps because he also had a very busy social life. According to a fellow student who'd studied with him—how on earth had Harvey managed to find one so quickly?—Byron was a hit with the ladies, his friend claiming there were streams of them going in and out of his on-campus bedroom, despite it being against the rules.

Rules, Cleo decided somewhat cynically, would not apply to the son and heir of the Maddox Media Empire. Money would have greased palms and all rules would have gone out of the window. Not the girls, however. They wouldn't have climbed through the windows. They would have walked right through the front door.

Such thoughts reminded Cleo to keep her wits about her with this man. He wasn't to be taken lightly in business. But very lightly when it came to other matters. Byron claimed to want to get married and have children but his past history suggested he got cold feet whenever the reality of commitment came close to fruition. Harvey's reports on Byron's years of working with his father all over the world suggested there had been less bed-hopping than at university, but he'd rarely been seen without some very beautiful girl on his arm. And, no doubt, in his bed. Since returning to Sydney to live, he'd had several short-term girlfriends followed recently by two serious relationships, resulting in engagements.

But she already knew all about them, so Cleo skipped over that part of Harvey's report to inspect the section concerning Byron's business and financial details. Which was pretty well exactly as she expected. No mining investments. Most of Byron's money was in property, both commercial and domestic. Some airports figured as well. And then there were the holiday resorts, the retirement villages and the nursing homes. Nothing in the stock market. Not even the so-called blue-chip shares. He had invested in two movies—both of which had made him a profit—but there weren't any more of what she would call high-risk investments.

Once again, Cleo wondered how Harvey had found out so much about Byron in such a short space of time. Scott called Harvey an IT genius, with more tech savvy than several of those young Silicon Valley experts. Yet Harvey wasn't at all young, and didn't look anything like a computer nerd. More like an aging bikie, being big and bald and beefy, with a penchant for leather jackets.

Cleo flipped her phone shut and glanced over at Byron, who'd sunk down in his chair, arms crossed, eyes firmly shut.

A glance at her watch said they'd been in the air only forty minutes. Still over two hours to go.

She sighed.

'I'm not asleep,' Byron said, his eyelids lifting. 'I never can sleep on planes.'

'Me, either.' Not that she'd been on that many. Only domestic flights.

Byron unwrapped his arms and stood up abruptly. 'Come on, let's go watch a movie.' And he stretched out his hand to her.

'A movie?' Cleo echoed as she put her hand in his and let him draw her to her feet.

'Dad's got all the latest movies. Movies and television are a good chunk of his business nowadays. That's why he got this plane decked out with a home theatre, so that he can watch the latest releases whilst he flies across the Pacific, or wherever.'

Cleo tried to concentrate on what Byron was saying and not the tingling heat his touch generated in her hand. And up her arm.

'He obviously doesn't sleep much on flights either, then,' she said as Byron led her along to the large cream sofa that ran along the wall opposite a huge flat-screen TV.

'Not much.' He saw her settled on the sofa, then went over to slip a DVD into the built-in player. 'He was also missing his wife on this last trip over,' he added as he straightened then turned to face Cleo. 'Alexandra didn't want to bring her new baby all this way for just two weeks. Dad's here to put his harbourside mansion on the market. He reckons if he visits Sydney in future, he'll stay in a hotel. Right!' he said, turning back briefly to press play. 'This is a romantic comedy that a rival company of Dad's produced late last year. It's not actually out yet but apparently there's a real buzz about it. We watched it together on the way over and neither of us liked it much. It'll be good to get a female opinion. Now, I'll just rustle up some movie snacks whilst you start watching.'

'Okay,' she said, glad to have some mental distraction for the thoughts that kept going through her head. It was a struggle to dismiss the notion that Byron did actually like her. And liked her company. Maybe he hadn't asked her to go to his mother's birthday party just to protect himself from predatory women. Maybe he was actually attracted to her.

And maybe you're living in a fantasy world, Cleo Shelton. Why should he be attracted to someone who looks like you do? You've seen photos of his ex-fiancées. Even if Grace performs a makeover miracle, you won't hold a candle to a supermodel, or a beautiful actress.

Cleo glanced down at her own outfit. She wished with all her heart that she'd worn something nicer, instead of these old jeans and the same jacket she'd worn yesterday. She'd believed her clothes were suitable for a visit to a dusty old refinery, but now they just felt dated and dismal.

It was at that moment Cleo vowed to do something about her entire wardrobe. She would get Grace's advice, not just for a party dress but for everything else, from casual gear to the latest fashions for work. She would probably still lean towards pant suits to wear to the office. But ones with more style, matched with more colourful tops. Maybe even some silk scarves. She'd always admired women who accessorised their outfits with long silk scarves.

'So what do you think so far?' Byron asked when he returned to the sofa with a huge bowl of microwaved popcorn.

She could hardly venture a reasoned opinion, since she hadn't actually been watching.

'It's okay so far,' she said. 'Mighty fine breakfast you've got there.'

When he grinned over at her, her stomach did a total somersault. Under the circumstances, Cleo did the only thing she could think of. She focused on watching the movie. And thankfully so did he. Byron didn't say another word till the credits started to roll.

'Well?' he said, putting aside the now empty bowl.

'It's very ordinary,' she replied. 'A cheap version of *Pretty Woman*, but with no star quality and none of the other movie's appeal.'

'Wow,' Byron said, and stared at her. 'Neither Dad nor I knew what was wrong with it, but you hit the nail right on the head.'

'That's only my opinion, remember. Someone else might think very differently. An American audience might like it very much. I'm not overly fond of slapstick humour. I always think it's a cheap way to get laughs. The comedy should come from the characters, not the girl dropping hot coffee in the guy's lap. What's funny about that? I know the waitress is supposed to be a klutz, but being a klutz isn't an attractive trait. It's dumb. She'd be fired in the real world. Aside from that, the plot is very devicey and not believable. I mean, would a billionaire really have his breakfast every morning in such a dreary café? Not only that, this kind of movie is supposed to be about the underdog girl being swept away into a world of wealth and glamour. That didn't happen. He comes down to her level, not the other way around. I doubt it's going to be a big success. What's it called? I missed the title.'

His smile was wide. 'It's called *The Girl in the Café*.'

'You have to be kidding me.'

'Nope. I think they're trying to cash in on all the recent movie successes which had girl in the title.'

'But they're all thrillers, not romantic comedies.'

'I know. What would you call it?'

'I have no idea. I don't think any title would save it. The only good thing about it is the soundtrack.'

'I think Dad should hire you as a consultant. Or I will. Either way, you're wasted working for a mining company.'

'But I love working for Scott,' she countered, despite being thrilled by Byron's praise.

'You could work for us, part-time. After hours,' he added, and gave her a look that sent a decidedly sexual shiver ricocheting down her spine.

'We've begun our descent into Townsville, Mr Maddox,' the pilot suddenly announced over the intercom. 'Time to buckle up.'

'Have I time for a quick dash to the bathroom?' Cleo asked, trying to ignore her still-racing heartbeat.

'Sure.'

Ten minutes later they were on the ground. At least, the plane was. An increasingly infatuated Cleo was still up there in cloud land. Or La-La Land, as Doreen called it. The place where the brain ceased to work, leaving nothing but a blank mind and a body that responded on instinct. When Byron put his hand on her elbow to guide her to the plane's exit, that electric charge once again raced up her arm. Cleo's head automatically turned to look at him. Partly in puzzlement. Partly in a dazed wonder. He looked back, his own eyes narrowing slightly when she stood there, not moving, just staring at him.

It took a few seconds before her brain kicked back into gear.

Don't make something out of good manners, Cleo. And don't, for pity's sake, start making a fool of yourself over this man.

'It's quite warm up here, isn't it?' she said with a cool smile, after which she made her way down the steps to the hot tarmac, and the hire car already waiting for them.

CHAPTER NINE

THE HIRE CAR was an SUV. Silver, with grey leather seats and a driver named Lou. He was also a talker, but not irritatingly so. A blessing in disguise, Byron soon decided, since Cleo seemed to have fallen oddly silent once they climbed in the back of the car. He liked the way she'd talked to him on the plane. Liked her warm smiles and sparkling eyes.

They weren't sparkling now. They were cool and businesslike, and mostly directed through the passenger window. Frankly, he couldn't quite work Cleo out. Which annoyed him. He was usually good at working out women.

Or was he?

If he was such a good judge of the opposite sex, then he should have realised earlier that both Eva and Simone were little better than gold-diggers. Sure, they both had careers of their own, but the bitter truth was they wanted the bonus—or the back-up—of being married to money. He wouldn't mind betting that neither of them would have rushed into giving him the children he craved. Eva would not have wanted to risk spoiling her figure. Simone might have given in and had one child, eventually, but only as an insurance policy. Ex-wives with children got a better divorce settlement than those without.

'I presume you folks want to have a bite to eat before going out to the refinery?' Lou asked once they left the airport. 'Or did you eat on the plane?'

'Nothing substantial,' Byron said. 'But we don't have time to linger. It would have to be quick. What would you suggest?'

'There's a nice little café on the way out of town. It's rarely crowded and they do a mean club sandwich. And their coffee is great. Would that do?'

'What do you say, Cleo?' he asked her, forcing her to turn back to face him.

'Sounds like just the thing,' she replied with a stiff little smile.

Byron frowned. What had he possibly done to upset her?

She remained annoyingly cool during their stop at the café, hardly saying a word as he devoured his sandwich whilst she ate slowly and thoughtfully. Thank goodness he'd insisted Lou sit and have something to eat with them otherwise the table would have been a desert of conversation.

'I used to work at the refinery,' Lou said as he munched away.

Byron put down the small remainder of his sandwich. 'And?' he prodded.

'Great place to work.'

'So why did you leave?' he persisted, at which point Cleo put down her sandwich and looked up.

Lou shrugged. 'I could see the writing on the wall,' he said. 'No more bonuses at Christmas. Prices falling. The boss looking worried. So I thought I'd jump ship before the whole thing sank.'

'I see,' Byron said. 'So you don't suggest I come on board at this point in time?'

Lou looked alarmed. 'Hell, you're not thinking of buying the place, are you?'

'Not sure yet.'

'Bloody hell. I was told you were a big shot movie maker. I thought you must have been going to make a film out here or something. I thought you might be looking for a location, not an investment.'

Byron smiled in dry amusement. 'Afraid not.'

Lou pulled a face. 'I hope I haven't spoken out of turn,' he said, glancing from Byron to Cleo, then back to Byron.

'Absolutely not,' Byron reassured the man. 'I already knew the refinery was in financial difficulty. But it's good to get the local perspective as well. And I rather like your idea about a movie set up here. I'll certainly give it some thought.'

'Great.'

'Drink up, then,' Byron said, lifting his own coffee mug. 'Time we were on the road again.'

The road wasn't too bad, and the countryside was quite beautiful. Until they hit mining country, at which point the trees disappeared, and the land was scraped clean. Great piles of earth dotted the landscape, in the middle of which stood the refinery, its great smoke stacks reaching into the sky. No smoke, however. Nothing was doing that day.

Once through the security gates, they drove past lots of utilitarian buildings. The largest one had *'Canteen'* written above the door. Everything looked a bit...be-draggled, like Detroit after the car industry moved out. The manager of the refinery put on a good show, but Byron could see past his bonhomie to the worried man beneath. A quick tour of the refinery was followed by lots of excuses why it wasn't in production that day, none of which Byron bought. Cleo didn't accompany him on the tour for longer than five minutes, claiming a head-ache, which Byron only half believed. She'd apologised, then retreated to the canteen for water and painkillers.

So Byron was surprised to see her hunched down in the dirt outside the canteen, inspecting the back left foot of what had to be the biggest, ugliest dog he'd ever seen. Maybe a cross between a Labrador and a Great Dane, with a bit of dingo and donkey thrown in for good measure.

'What's that you've got there, Cleo?' he asked as he walked over to her, the manager in tow.

Her face scrunched up as she straightened. 'He's got something wrong with his leg. He was limping very badly. But I can't find anything. His foot's fine, but he doesn't like to put his weight on that back leg. He keeps holding it up.'

'That's Mungo,' the manager said. 'He's been limp-ing for a good while.'

'Then why hasn't he been taken to a vet?' Cleo de-manded to know, clearly outraged.

The manager shrugged. 'He's not my dog. He doesn't belong to anyone. He just showed up one day a few weeks ago. The men called him Mungo because he's a mongrel. They give him some food every now and then, and the girls in the canteen make sure he has a bucket of water.'

'But he needs to go to a vet,' Cleo insisted. 'The poor thing's in pain.'

'He'll get better,' the manager said dismissively.

'No, he won't, actually,' Byron intervened, a few things clicking together in his brain. 'Not if he's ruptured his cruciate ligament.'

'His what?' both Cleo and the manager chorused.

'His cruciate ligament. It's an injury which is quite common with big dogs. If they don't get it fixed, they'll always limp, then have severe arthritis as they get older. My sister has a golden retriever who suffered the same fate a couple of years ago. We had it operated on and Jasper's just fine now.'

'Better to have him put down, then,' the manager said, at which point the dog looked up, his dark eyes unbearably sad. Cleo's weren't much better.

Please, they said, looking down at the dog, then right at *him*.

Byron sighed. 'If you can find him an owner,' he said to her, 'I'll take him to Sydney with us and have him operated on.'

Her eyes lit up like the Harbour Bridge on New Year's Eve. 'That would be marvellous. And Doreen and I will take him.'

Byron frowned. 'Who's Doreen?'

'My mother-in-law. She lives with me.'

Byron absorbed that information with a smidgeon of dismay. He'd rather liked the thought that Cleo might not

have been happy in her marriage. But you didn't live with
your mother-in-law if you'd hated her son, did you? Not
that it really mattered. He wasn't going to get caught up
in Cleo's emotional baggage, was he?

'He'll need to be kept quiet for a long while after
the operation,' he warned. 'He can't be allowed to run
around, or go up and down a lot of steps, not until it's
all healed.'

'That's okay. My place only has one step at the front
and back. And Doreen isn't working at the moment.'

'Okay. That's all settled, then. Where's Lou?'

'He's in the canteen,' Cleo told him.

'Then go get him,' he commanded as he scooped the
dog up in his arms the way he'd learned to do with Jasper. 'And we'll get going.'

'It'll cost you a fortune, mate,' the manager warned
as he walked with Byron to the parked SUV.

'I know,' came his rueful reply. Around five grand at
this particular hospital. And counting.

But you only got what you paid for in life. And it
wasn't as though he couldn't afford it. Plus, it was going
to make him a hero in Cleo's eyes.

Not much a woman wouldn't do for her hero...

CHAPTER TEN

DOREEN WAS STILL up when Cleo finally arrived home that evening.

'Ah, you're home,' she said, glancing up from where she was curled up on their very comfy sofa, dressed in her pale blue dressing gown and fluffy slippers. 'Long day?'

'You could say that.' Cleo had eventually sent Doreen a text on the flight home to explain that she wasn't staying in Townsville overnight, but that she was coming home that day. She didn't say anything about Mungo at that stage, feeling the dog situation was better explained in person. Apparently, Doreen hadn't noticed her overnight bag sitting next to the front door, which was typical of Doreen. She would make a terrible witness to a crime.

'I'll make you a hot chocolate,' she offered immediately, uncurling herself and heading for the kitchen.

'That would be lovely,' Cleo said, and followed her.

The kitchen wasn't large but it was well appointed, and had a breakfast bar with three stools at which Doreen and Cleo ate most of their meals—unlike when she'd lived there with Martin, who had always insisted on eating in the more formal dining room, even at break-fast. Cleo dumped her handbag on the floor and climbed up onto one of the stools.

'I can't imagine you had much success,' Doreen said as she made hot chocolate for two. 'The mining indus-try is in the doldrums.'

'I seriously doubt Byron is going to become Scott's new business partner,' Cleo admitted with a touch of sadness. 'Which is a pity. Scott could do with a partner who can be ruthless when he needs to be. Byron told me on the flight home that the nickel refinery needs to be closed down straight away, and I agree with him. But you know Scott. He *says* he's going to shut it down but he's got a soft heart and can't bear to lay people off until he's tried everything possible.'

Doreen sighed. 'I know. I wish he was *my* boss. Then I might still have a job.'

Until recently, Doreen had worked at a local su-permarket. But when their business had started to go downhill due to some poor business decisions and fierce competition from a nearby rival, she was laid off.

'I get so bored sometimes,' Doreen added, and pushed Cleo's mug over to her.

'What would you think about getting a dog?' she asked, not sure how Doreen was going to react. She'd never had a dog, her husband not allowing it. Or so she'd confided to her one day. The same had applied to Martin. He wouldn't even let Cleo get a cat. He wasn't an animal hater. But he'd hated anything that took Cleo's attention away from him. She wondered suddenly if that had been the real reason he'd kept putting off having a baby…

'Oh, I don't know,' Doreen said. 'Some dogs can be very smelly.'

Cleo thought of the doggy pong that had invaded the SUV, and then the plane, Byron complaining that he would have to have the jet thoroughly cleaned and fumigated before handing it back to his father. But his complaints had been light-hearted, a laugh hidden behind his poker face. The nurse at the Sydney veterinary hospital they'd taken him to had said she would have to bathe him and vaccinate first before they could proceed with the operation the following day.

Byron had certainly done his part. Now it was Cleo's job to convince Doreen that they both needed a dog.

'True,' Cleo said. 'But they're not called man's best friend for nothing. They give unconditional love.' And if there were two women in the world who needed unconditional love it was them!

Doreen finally twigged that there was something in the air besides idle speculation. Her eyes narrowed as she looked at Cleo.

'I might be imagining things but I have a feeling that something is going on here. Come on, Cleo. Don't beat about the bush. If you're thinking about buying a dog, then just say so.'

'I'm not thinking about *buying* a dog. Mungo is more of a rescue dog.'

'Mungo,' Doreen repeated with a wince. 'Why do I get the feeling that we're not talking about some cute little puppy?'

Cleo decided that a picture was worth a thousand words, so she bent down and pulled her phone out of her bag and showed Doreen a few snaps she'd taken of Mungo sprawled across the leather sofa in Byron's jet, then a couple more on the way to the vet as she cradled his big head in her lap in the back of Byron's car.

Fortunately, one of the snaps captured the sadness in his large soulful eyes and not just his great big ugly body.

'Oh, the poor darling,' Doreen said, sniffling a little. She was a soft touch, was Doreen.

After that, Cleo felt free to tell her everything, including how wonderful Byron had been about the dog. He'd insisted on paying for the operation, excusing his generosity by saying he could easily afford it. But really, that wasn't the point. A lot of rich men could afford to do a lot of things but they rarely did them. Most men in Byron's position wouldn't have cared, let alone gone to so much trouble. And it had certainly been trouble, lugging Mungo around.

But Cleo couldn't expect him to do any more than he had already done. From now on it was up to her and Doreen to do everything, which included picking up Mungo on Saturday afternoon. Knowing that he wouldn't fit in the back of her small car, Cleo had already decided to ask Harvey to help. He wouldn't mind. He was footloose and fancy-free, having been divorced for years, and with no live-in partner that she knew of. He also had a huge SUV that would easily accommodate Mungo.

Of course, it would be Doreen who accompanied Harvey to the vet's on Saturday afternoon, not her, since she would be busy getting herself dolled up for Byron's party that night. Which reminded her, Doreen knew nothing of this development. No doubt she'd be surprised, but happy enough, Cleo thought. She was always telling Cleo that she should go out more. It had been *her* idea for Cleo to start dating!

As it turned out, Doreen wasn't just surprised. She was shocked.

'Are you telling me that this billionaire you spent today with has asked you to go to his mother's birthday party with him?'

'Um… Yes.'

'But why? I mean… Oh, Lord, that sounded awful but—'

'It's all right, Doreen,' Cleo cut in. 'I asked him exactly the same question.'

'And what did he say?'

'Apparently, his mother is a meddling matchmaker who is always trying to set up potential brides for him to meet.'

'Oh, I see. And he doesn't want to get married.'

'Actually, he does. Just not to the type of women his mother likes.'

Doreen gave her a sharp look. 'You seem to have learned a lot about this man in one day.'

'Well, I did go to lunch with him on Wednesday as well, remember?'

'That was just a business lunch. This sounds like a lot more than business. Are you sure he doesn't fancy you?'

Cleo wished she hadn't blushed.

'And you fancy him, don't you?'

She could have denied it, but what was the point?

'Oh, dear,' Doreen said with a sigh. 'As much as I would love to see you move on, Cleo, I don't think someone like this Byron is the way to go. You wouldn't fit in with his crowd, would you? I mean, men like that. They date seriously beautiful women.'

'I said that to him too. He said I would look stunning if I wore the right clothes and had myself done over in a beauty salon.'

Had he actually used the word 'stunning'? Probably not. More like *just fine*.

'Heavens!' Doreen exclaimed. 'And are you going to do all that?'

'I certainly am. And I'm going to buy a totally new wardrobe, not just one new dress. I'm sick to death of the way I look, Doreen. It's time to change.'

'But where will you start? You don't have a clue about fashion.'

Cleo had to laugh. 'Neither do you.'

Doreen smiled a strange, sad smile. 'I did. Once. Until I got married and my brand-new husband cut up all my really nice clothes, then he cut off all my lovely long hair. He said he didn't like his wife looking like a slut.'

Cleo gasped.

'After that, he chose all my clothes, and I never grew my hair. By the time he died, I had lost all interest in what I wore, or how I looked.'

Cleo felt tears prick at her eyes. Martin hadn't been as bad as that. But then he hadn't had to be. She'd already dressed like a middle-aged spinster when they met. All he'd had to do was compliment the way she looked and she'd just kept on dressing the same way.

'Then maybe it's time for you to change too,' Cleo said. 'We'll go clothes shopping together tomorrow.

Grace can help you buy a new wardrobe at the same time.'

'Who's Grace?'

'She's Byron's PA. Trust me when I say she has a lot of style know-how.'

'But doesn't she have to work tomorrow?'

'Byron contacted her during the flight home and gave her the day off to help me. He's playing golf with some movie producer so she isn't needed to be on deck.'

'Doesn't sound like he works too hard,' Doreen said with a cynical edge.

'Actually, he told me he hates golf but the guy he's playing with likes to do business over a game.'

Another sharp look from Doreen. 'What else do you know about this man?'

Cleo smiled. 'He doesn't eat breakfast, he's an awful judge of movies and rather ruthless in business. But underneath his bachelor playboy façade, he's really very sweet. And very kind.'

Doreen rolled her eyes. 'Of all the people for you to fall for.'

Cleo laughed. 'I haven't fallen for him. I just like him.'

And I want to go to bed with him. Oh, yes. I want to go to bed with him a lot!

CHAPTER ELEVEN

'YOU'VE BEEN HAVING putting lessons.'

Byron glanced up at Blake after he extracted his golf ball from the sixteenth hole. 'Not exactly. Grace gave me a few tips.'

'Grace?'

'My PA.'

'Have I met Grace?'

'Probably.'

'Is she young, blonde, and beautiful?'

'No, that's Jackie. She's my receptionist. Grace *is* blonde, but she's in her late forties. Let me also add that both women are taken. Jackie is engaged and Grace is coming up for her twenty-fifth wedding anniversary.'

Blake snorted. 'That would have to be a record these days.'

'It is a rare achievement. I'll grant you that.'

'So what happened with you and the gorgeous Simone?' Blake asked as they pulled their buggies over to the seventeenth tee.

Byron shrugged. 'I realised that I'd never make it with her to my *first* wedding anniversary, let alone the twenty-fifth.'

'Ambitious young actresses are never a good bet, Byron. Not in the marriage department. Trust me, I know. I was married to one of them. For about ten minutes. They are terribly good fakers, until they've got your ring on their finger. Better for men like us to stay single.'

Byron knew exactly what Blake meant. A happy marriage was a rare thing amongst the very wealthy. After his parents' divorce, his father had taken many years to find Alexandra. Fortunately, she was wealthy in her own right and didn't need Lloyd Maddox's money.

'But I want to get married,' Byron said. 'And I want to have children. I just have to find the right woman.'

'Well, good luck with that. Now are we going to get back to the business at hand?' he asked as they stopped by the seventeenth tee.

Just then the sun came out from behind a cloud, bathing the course in the kind of unseasonal warmth that late autumn often brought to Sydney. Tomorrow the first of June would herald the coming of winter. Fortunately, the forecast for the weekend was for further sunny days, though the mornings would be crisp. Byron knew his mother's party would spill out to the spacious pool area so rain would have been a disappointment to her. Not that people would be swimming. But the pool did make for an impressive backdrop for her myriad celebrity guests. Byron loved his mother but she could be a terrible snob.

It was as well that Cleo was having a makeover, or Rosalind would have looked down her nose at her, and wondered what on earth Byron was doing with such a drab creature. His mother wouldn't have understood that he had liked Cleo from the first, despite her boring wardrobe and her lack of artifice. Though maybe it was *because* of those very factors that he liked her so much. He wondered suddenly if he would like her quite so much when she was all dolled up.

How perverse would it be if he didn't?

'It's your honour since you won the last hole,' Blake pointed out irritably when Byron made no move to tee up. 'Which reminds me. If you want to invest in my next movie it might be wise to lose a hole or two. As it stands, I'm one shot behind.'

Byron laughed. 'That's what Grace said. But you know what, Blake? I don't really give a damn if you let me invest in your next movie or not,' he said off-handedly, having found the best way to do business with some men was not to seem eager.

Blake scowled, his dark brows drawing together. He had the looks of a tyrant, with gleaming black hair, a darkly brooding face and piercing blue eyes that bored into you. Handsome, though. And amazingly young to be on the cusp of conquering Hollywood. Only thirty.

'Why not?' he demanded to know.

'Quite frankly, I have another potential investment on my plate at the moment, one which might cost me a good chunk of money. Not sure I will have enough spare cash left over to risk on a movie.'

Blake's face darkened further, if that were possible. *'Risk?'* His eyes scorched Byron with their fury. 'It's not a *risk* to invest in one of my movies. They've all made money.'

'True. But now you're off to Hollywood and the big boys over there are sure to influence you. You won't be truly independent for long.'

'Rubbish! I will always do my own thing!'

Byron teed up then whacked the ball right down the middle of the fairway. Though not as far as he was capable of. 'Maybe I could manage to rustle up a million or two,' he said casually, then dumped his driver back into his bag.

'I'm going to need more than that,' Blake grumped.

'How much, then?'

'Twenty million at least. My next film is going to be a blockbuster.'

Byron laughed. 'See what I mean? You're thinking like a Hollywood producer already.'

Blake speared him with a steely eye. 'Look, are you in or out?'

'Is Lachlan Rodgers going to be in it?'

'He certainly is. I've already signed him up for the main role.'

'In that case, I'm in. That boy has star quality written all over him.'

'He certainly has. And it's *me* who's made him a star.' Looking satisfied, Blake teed off and drove his ball a good fifty yards past Byron's.

As both men collected their buggies and strolled down the fairway, a more relaxed Blake turned to Byron. 'So, are you dating anyone special at the moment?'

Byron gave the matter a moment's thought before answering.

'Yes. Actually, I am,' he admitted. His mother's birthday party wasn't going to be the last time he saw Cleo. Hopefully.

'Could she be the wife you're looking for?'

'I don't think so.'

'Just a fill-in, then,' Blake said. 'Until the right girl comes along.'

Byron didn't like Cleo being described that way. She'd become way more than just a fill-in. If truth be told, his mind was obsessing over her to such an extent that he was finding it hard to sleep at night. He thought of all he had done yesterday, just to impress her. If he'd been visiting the refinery alone, that mangy dog would have been left up there. But no, Cleo had been with him, and he simply could not resist her pleading eyes and soft heart. So he'd loaded the smelly damned animal onto his father's plane and brought him back to Sydney, then taken him to the vet and handed over his credit card details to have 'darling' Mungo operated on and looked after. All to see the joy—and the gratitude—in Cleo's quite lovely brown eyes. Now he was even thinking of becoming a partner in McAllister Mines, just so he could keep on seeing her. Which was insane!

Maybe if he could manage to seduce her tomorrow night as he'd originally intended, then he could start thinking with his brain again instead of his—

It had steered him wrong in the past and was probably doing the same again.

Yet it wasn't just sex he wanted from Cleo any more, was it? He enjoyed being with her. It was a first for him where women were concerned. God, that made him sound so shallow. And chauvinistic. He *knew* there was much more to the opposite sex then just sex. He'd met plenty of super-smart women in his life. Career girls with more degrees than he had.

The trouble was when this type of woman met *him* she strangely forgot all personal ambition and started coming on to him big-time, making it obvious that he could have her whenever and wherever he wanted. So of course he usually accommodated her wishes—if she was beautiful as well—without bothering to get to know her first.

His ex-fiancées, however, had played their cards a little better. Eva hadn't jumped into bed with him for at least a fortnight after their first meeting, whetting his appetite with her gorgeous body and elusive tactics. She hadn't been that fabulous in bed once he'd got her there, but by then he'd been so excited by the chase that any sex would have felt fantastic. Eva was also an expert flatterer, telling him she'd never had better and that she was madly in love with him. A month later they'd been engaged, at which point Eva had started showing her true colours, expecting him to spend a small fortune on an engagement ring, not to mention weekends away at luxury resorts and dinner every other night at the most expensive restaurants. When she'd had to go away to Hawaii on a photographic shoot for a fortnight, Byron had found that he hadn't missed her at all.

It had been the beginning of the end.

Simone, admittedly, *had* jumped into bed with him a lot sooner than Eva. The very first night they'd met, in fact. Her skill was that she was *very* adventurous where sex was concerned. And seemingly insatiable. Easy for a man to become addicted to sex like that, and to believe her declarations of undying love. Until that million-dollar engagement ring had been on her finger. After that, the sex had started to dry up, and so had the love he'd thought he felt for her.

Both women had been very angry when he broke up with them. But Byron knew what had angered them most was that they'd overestimated the power of their physical beauty, and underestimated Byron's desire to marry a woman who would deliver the happy and settled family life he craved.

In hindsight, he hated that he'd even considered marrying either of them.

Byron knew that Cleo would never play those kinds of games. As Grace had said, she was a *nice* girl. Perhaps this was partly because she wasn't *obviously* sexy as Eva and Simone were. But, strangely, he found that he admired that. He admired *her*. And he desired her. Very much so.

Tomorrow night could not come quickly enough. He wondered if he should ring her, see how she and Grace were doing.

Maybe after the game…

Cleo, Doreen and Grace were relaxing over coffee and salad wraps at an alfresco café in Martin Place, numerous plastic bags at their feet, when Cleo's phone rang, her eyebrows arching when she saw it was Byron calling.

'It's Byron,' she told the others before she answered.

When both women gave her a knowing look, she rolled her eyes at them, then stood up to walk away from their table to take the call.

'Hi there,' she answered brightly. Lord, but just hearing his voice gave her a lift. 'I thought you'd still be on the golf course.'

'Blake's a fast player. We're in the club house, having lunch. He's at the bar, getting us both a beer, so I thought I'd give you a quick ring, see how you and Grace are going.'

'Very good. Actually, Doreen is with us too. She needed some fashion advice as well.'

'Well, Grace is an expert.'

'Which I have you to thank for. And I do. Wholeheartedly. Grace really knows her stuff, doesn't she?' Cleo was thrilled with what she'd already bought. And they hadn't finished yet. It was only just after noon.

'Grace is my secret weapon. You know what they say—behind every successful man is a seriously smart woman.'

'She's very nice, too.'

'Indeed she is. Okay. Blake's on his way back. I'll pick you up at seven-thirty tomorrow evening. Try to be ready,' he said. 'It's a long drive from Leichardt to Palm Beach.'

Cleo swallowed. It was one thing to buy some fabulous new clothes, quite another to wear them with the kind of panache she wanted to show off with tomorrow night.

'I'll be ready,' she choked out with a sudden dip of confidence.

'Good. And you've got someone to pick up the dog tomorrow?'

'Yes. That's all settled.' Which was just as well, since

she would be spending most of tomorrow getting the works at the exclusive beauty salon Grace had booked. She'd been lucky there'd been a last-minute cancellation.

'Great,' Byron said. 'Have to go.'

'Before you do, did you win?' Cleo asked.

'Of course not. I'm not an idiot. But you can tell Grace that I putted well. *Au revoir.*'

'Byron said to tell you that he didn't win,' Cleo reported as she sat back down at their table. 'But that he putted well.'

Grace laughed.

Cleo frowned. 'Do you think he deliberately lost?'

'Possibly.'

'But…'

'All's fair in love and business, Cleo,' Grace said with a pragmatic shrug. 'Byron wants a part of Fantasy Productions. It never does to antagonise a man you want to do business with, especially one with an ego as huge as Blake Randall.'

'True,' Cleo murmured, thinking that it was just as well she'd said yes to going to Byron's party. Though to be honest, her priority was no longer getting him to invest in McAllister Mines. She just wanted to spend more time with him. Of course, if he did invest in McAllister Mines, she *would* spend more time with him. But if she were strictly honest, the fate of Scott's business was a long way from her mind today. The fate she was more interested in was her own.

Her sigh carried a degree of frustration. Because she still wasn't convinced that all the expense she was going to would be worth it. She would never look remotely as good as that Simone creature. Or that other one. Eva What's-her-name. Both of them had exuded serious sex appeal. She didn't even know *how* to exude sex appeal.

'No point being tired,' Grace said, misinterpreting her sigh. 'We have heaps to do yet. Lingerie to buy. And shoes. And bags. Not to mention perfume. Come on, we'll go up to the David Jones store on Elizabeth Street where we can get them to mind these parcels whilst we shop till we drop. Then, when we're finished, I'll call a taxi to take you home. No catching the train with all you'll have to carry!'

CHAPTER TWELVE

'THANK GOD,' BYRON muttered when he turned into Cleo's street and saw a car leaving. It was only a short street, but the houses were long and narrow, so there were plenty of them. And plenty of occupants, obviously. This was the inner western suburbs after all. And Sydney was a city of car owners.

He backed into the blessedly empty space, checking his watch before he climbed out from behind the wheel. Seven-thirty exactly.

The night was on the cool side, he noted as he zapped the car locked. He had settled on a lightweight, casually tailored suit in pale grey, which had loose-fitting trousers and a one-button jacket—which he always left open—teaming it with a crew-necked white top, rather than a normal shirt. His shoes and belt were black, locally made in crocodile skin. Byron liked to support Australian manufacture. The suit, however, was Italian; he only wore the best, after all.

An uncharacteristic tension gripped his insides as he made his way down the side path of the small wooden house to the front door. Possibly it was the residue of his thought yesterday that he might not like Cleo as much once Grace had finished with her. Or perhaps it was this afternoon's text from Grace telling him that he was in for a big surprise when he picked Cleo up.

There was no doubt that his PA was enjoying this situation enormously. Though why, he wasn't sure. Maybe she'd inherited the same matchmaking gene that his mother had. Or maybe all women were addicted to romantic endings. Byron knew there would be no romantic ending for himself and Cleo. A romantic interlude, perhaps, but they certainly weren't destined for happily-ever-after.

Still, that didn't mean they couldn't have a very satisfying affair.

Strangely, this thought didn't satisfy Byron as much as it originally had. It worried him that he was already becoming emotionally involved with this woman. He didn't want to fall in love with Cleo. But he had an awful feeling that he just might, if he kept on seeing her after tonight.

Another perverse thought.

Damn, damn and double damn!

Taking a deeply gathering breath, he let it out then rang the doorbell, which brought a volley of loud barking from inside the house, followed by Cleo telling Mungo in a calm but firm voice to be quiet; that he wasn't to worry; that it was just Byron. The dog fell silent just as the front door was swept open.

The words *big surprise* did not begin to describe Byron's reaction to the woman standing before him. If he hadn't looked into her very familiar brown eyes, he would not have recognised her. Her gorgeous hair was down, waving around her face and shoulders like a movie star from the old days. Ava Gardner sprang to mind. Her face was perfectly made up, enhancing the beauty that was already there, waiting to be highlighted. Her red-glossed mouth looked lush and seductive, her eyes even larger now that she was wearing eyeliner and mascara. Some blush enhanced her cheekbones and gave her features more definition.

But it was what she was wearing that stunned Byron the most. Her outfit was made in an electric-blue slinky material, showing off her hourglass shape, and skimming over her gorgeously full breasts. Her shoes were gold high-heeled sandals, which showed slender ankles and red toenails. Her fingernails were painted too, but not red. They were an elegant, pale pink. She wore no jewellery but there was a tantalising perfume wafting from her delicious-looking body. It smelled faintly of vanilla, and other scents he couldn't identify.

He looked her up and down with overt admiration. And yes, a wild burst of sheer lust. By the time his gaze returned to her face, her eyes seemed to have grown even bigger, a touching look of vulnerability in their widening depths. He suspected that Cleo was still feeling a little unsure, despite the incredible transformation.

'I'm so sorry,' he said, straight-faced. 'I must have come to the wrong address. I was expecting Cleo Shelton to answer the door.'

Her face immediately broke into a wide smile. 'Don't be silly,' she said, but he could see she was pleased by his back-handed compliment. 'It's me.'

'You look stunning, Cleo. People will wonder what you're doing with me, not the other way around.'

'Oh, rubbish. You look incredible, like you always do.'

'You're too kind,' he said. 'Shall we go?' And he held out his arm.

'Could you possibly come in for a sec? Doreen's dying to meet you.'

Cleo's mother-in-law was younger than Byron had been picturing. And surprisingly attractive. She was wearing a maroon velvet tracksuit, and was seated on a dark blue sofa with Mungo sprawled out on the rug, his head on her foot. His bad back leg had been substantially shaved and there was a huge bandage wrapped around it, the same way Jasper's had been. The dog eyed Byron with suspicion, as though he knew he wasn't the hero both Cleo and Doreen seemed to think he was. Byron told Doreen not to get up, bending to give her a peck on the cheek and praising her for taking the dog in.

'Not everyone would have,' he said. Mungo gave him another slant-eyed look before ignoring him completely. Smart animals, dogs. They could spot real heroes from the pretend ones. Or the ones who had other not so heroic agendas.

Shut up, he told that voice in his head. *I won't do anything she doesn't want to do.*

'We'd better get going, Cleo,' he said when it looked as if Doreen was going to stare at him for ever.

'Don't forget your new purse,' Doreen blurted out to Cleo—her first words since Byron had walked in. 'And your keys. I won't wait up. I dare say you won't get home until late,' she directed at Byron, 'since the party's all the way up at Palm Beach.'

'True,' Byron replied whilst Cleo walked over to collect her new purse, a gold clutch, which was sitting on a nearby side table. Seeing her rear view as she walked in those sexy shoes did things to his body that made him glad his trousers weren't tight. He realised at that point he had no intention of staying at his mother's party until all hours. He wanted to spend time alone with Cleo. At his penthouse, preferably.

There was no use pretending that he could ignore the almost overwhelming desires that kept bubbling up as a result of her gorgeous transformation. Maybe he *was* shallow, because suddenly all he could think about was getting Cleo into bed. And keeping her there until he was well and truly satisfied. Still, at least being shallow was safer than falling in love with the woman. That wouldn't end well. And he was sick to death of wretched endings.

'Ready now?' he asked when she came up to him, purse in hand.

'As I'll ever be,' came her slightly nervous reply.

'You can't still be nervous,' he said once he had her in the car and they were safely under way. 'Not looking the way you do.'

'I am,' she confessed. 'I'm not sure I'll know what to say to the people there, especially your mother. I haven't been to a party in years.'

'Surely you go to your firm's Christmas parties.'

'That's not the same. I know everyone there. And I never stay late.'

'I see. Well, perhaps we won't stay too late at this one. We might go on somewhere else. Just you and me. Would you like that?'

What could she say? *I'd adore that?*

That would be way too telling. And potentially humiliating.

'Where were you thinking of taking me?' she asked, sounding as cool as a cucumber.

He slanted her a strangely surprised look. 'Where would you like to go?'

'I've heard the Opera House bar is lively on a Saturday night.' Someone had mentioned it, she couldn't remember who.

Byron pulled a face. 'It's always very crowded. You can't hear yourself think, let alone talk. I want to be alone with you, Cleo.'

Cleo sucked in a sharp breath. 'Why?' she blurted out before she could stop herself.

'You know why,' he said quietly.

'You…you want to have sex with me?' It sounded incredible once she'd said it out loud. Cleo knew she wanted to have sex with him but had never imagined her desire was returned.

Well, it hadn't been, had it? Not until you spent nearly six thousand dollars of your savings on transforming yourself into a presentable pretend girlfriend.

'Yes, of course I do.'

His casual admission took her breath away. It also angered her. So now she was fit to be seduced? Now that she looked good enough?

'I've wanted to have sex with you since thirty seconds after I met you,' he added with a rueful smile in his voice, and on his face.

If his earlier admission had taken her breath away, this one left her speechless.

'Are you going to say something?' he queried when she just sat there in a stunned silence for several seconds.

Cleo swallowed. 'I don't believe you,' she choked out. 'You couldn't possibly have. I looked dreadful that day.'

'You didn't look like you look tonight. That's true. But I still wanted you, Cleo. Trust me on that.'

'But why?'

'Why?' he echoed thoughtfully. 'Perhaps it was because I glimpsed the real you underneath the drab façade.'

'The real me?' What on earth was he talking about?

'The one who stared at me for a split second like I was a drink of water after a long and dusty desert trek.'

'Oh,' she said, embarrassed now. And yes, humiliated by the thought that he'd seen the instant attraction in her eyes. And yes, the craving.

'There's nothing more desirable,' he said, 'than a woman who wants you, despite herself.'

Cleo shook her head, scared by how intuitive he was. He'd read her like a book. Read her and played her.

'There's nothing wrong with wanting to have sex again, Cleo. It doesn't make your love for your husband any less real.'

Cleo stiffened, pressing her back and shoulders against the passenger seat. Her head turned to gaze out at the passing traffic. If only he knew...

But he would never know. Because she would never tell him.

When a sudden thought popped into her head, her eyes whipped back around to glare at him. 'You're not really interested in McAllister Mines, are you?' she said quite savagely. 'This was all just a game to you. A sex game.'

Byron hated the anger in her voice. And the hurt in her eyes.

But he hated himself more.

Okay, so it might have been a bit of a game to begin with. Hell, he'd *wanted* it to be just a game. But it wasn't any longer. Not totally. Underneath his lust, he genuinely cared about this woman and he wasn't going to do or say anything to hurt her further.

Glancing ahead, he saw that a corner was coming up. He turned down a side street and pulled abruptly over to the kerb. Once the engine was shut down, he twisted in his seat to face his startled passenger. She looked absolutely terrified, her eyes wide with shock, and confusion.

'Now let's get something straight, Cleo,' he said firmly. 'I *am* interested in McAllister Mines. But I'm more interested in *you*. Not just as a game, either. I told you the truth the other day. I like you and I like your company. And yes, I'd like to become your lover. The only lie I've told is the reason for asking you to accompany me to my mother's party. It wasn't to protect me from predatory females but because I wanted to be with you, and I didn't think you'd say yes to a straightforward invitation.'

'Really and truly?' she said, the words soft and breathless, her eyes still unsure.

'Oh, for pity's sake,' he growled, unsnapping his seat belt and reaching over to cup her face with his hands before bending his mouth to hers.

Cleo had thought endlessly about what it would be like to be kissed by Byron. But nothing had prepared her for the reality of his lips taking possession of hers. Or his tongue touching hers. Her chest immediately squeezed tight, a mushroom of sensation blooming in her stomach and exploding upwards and outwards, bringing with it a heat that threatened to make her self-combust. When the pressure of his mouth pushed her head back against the seat, she moaned, then opened her mouth wider, inviting him to a deeper invasion. His guttural groan of satisfaction did things to her that could only be described as wicked. She no longer cared what his motivations were. Or if he'd been lying just now. She wanted him even more than he wanted her. She was sure of it. Nothing mattered to Cleo in that moment except letting him know that she was his.

Have to stop kissing Cleo, Byron told himself a couple of minutes later. Lord, but she was like a drug. He'd kissed dozens of women before but none had made him feel what she was making him feel. All powerful. All man. All conquering. It took an enormous burst of willpower to tear his mouth away from hers.

Her eyes were closed, thankfully. Too bad about her lips, which remained tantalisingly parted and totally devoid of lipstick. As he stared down at the rapid rise and fall of her truly delicious chest, his body ached with the need to take things further. And soon. It pained him to think he had to go to his mother's birthday party, even for a short while. But he could hardly claim a last-minute illness. He'd already rung her to let her know he was on his way, and that he had a woman with him. She'd been intrigued, of course. Was this woman just a friend or someone new, someone…special? He'd laughed off her question and said she would have to wait and see for herself.

Yes, of course Cleo was someone special, he conceded. Very special indeed. Just not future wife special. So, it was best that he keep things sexual and superficial.

Byron's finger moved to trace her parted lips until her eyes opened, meeting his with vulnerability still in their depths.

'We won't spend too long at the party,' he told her as he returned to buckle back into his seat.

'All right,' she said, then sighed, as if she had no choice in the matter.

It bothered him, that sigh.

He speared her with an uncompromising glance. 'I won't ever ask you to do anything you don't want to do, Cleo.'

'Yes, I know,' she said. 'You're not that kind of man.'

He frowned. 'What kind am I?'

'Kind,' she said, smiling. 'Despite being dreadfully spoilt.'

He laughed. 'I really do like you, Cleo Shelton.'

'And I really like you, Byron Maddox,' she returned, still smiling.

'Really and truly?' he said, parodying her words earlier.

She reached over to smack him lightly on the arm. 'Don't you dare make fun of me. If you do I won't want to do *anything* with you.'

'Hell's bells!' he said, feigning shock horror. 'That would never do. Now we really do have to get going, or Mum will send out a search party.'

CHAPTER THIRTEEN

'OH, DEAR, I just realised something,' Cleo said when Byron announced that they were nearly there.

'What?'

'I didn't buy your mother a birthday present. Or even a card.' She'd been far too wrapped up all day in making herself over into the sort of woman Byron would date. Even *she* thought she looked pretty fabulous, but that didn't make her feel any less guilty over her selfishness.

'Don't stress about it,' Byron reassured her. 'I've bought her a gift, and a card. I'll say that they're from you as well.'

'Oh, thank you. That makes me feel better. What did you buy her?'

Byron's smile was wry. 'A book.'

Cleo frowned. 'That's *all*?' Hardly what she'd been imagining. Surely he could have afforded something a little more expensive—and imaginative—than a book.

Byron shrugged. 'I did have some very expensive flowers delivered today as well. Look, she's not an easy person to buy a present for. She doesn't like anyone to buy her clothes, or artwork, or anything for the house.

Husbands and lovers are allowed to buy women jewellery, but not a son. Or so she told me when I bought her a necklace once when I was a gauche teenager. But possibly that was because I didn't spend enough money on it. I bought her a lovely little sculpture last year—an original, might I add—and it now resides on the shelf behind the toilet in the pool house.'

'She has a pool house?'

'Yep. To go with the pool.'

'But she lives right on the beach.'

'The pool is more of a landscaping item than something Rosalind ever uses,' Byron explained. 'Lara swims in it occasionally. Though she prefers the beach. So does Jasper.' Cleo was glad she knew who he was talking about. Rosalind was his mother, Lara his teenage sister, and Jasper the golden retriever who'd had the same injury as Mungo.

'I doubt any of the guests will be swimming tonight,' Byron went on. 'The pool is heated, but the women won't want their hairstyles ruined. And the men will be more interested in the wine than anything else.'

Cleo didn't much like the sound of his mother's guests. Still, she wouldn't want her hairstyle ruined either. It had cost her a packet.

'So what was the book you bought?'

'The latest thriller by Daniel Silva. Mum loves him.'

'Then won't she have bought it herself?'

'Not yet. She actually doesn't buy books herself. She prefers to get books from the local library, then she doesn't feel obliged to finish one if she doesn't like it. She can be extravagant with some things but very frugal in other ways. Perhaps because she was once quite poor. Until she met my father, that is.'

'Are you saying she married him for his money? Is that why their marriage failed?' The questions fell out of her mouth before Cleo could stop herself. 'Sorry,' she said straight away. 'That was rude of me. And none of my business.'

'No, no, don't apologise. I think they were very much in love to begin with, but Dad was a workaholic and was away from home far too much. They just drifted apart, that's all. Ah, here we are at last.' And he turned into a narrow street that had wall-to-wall cars, with several parked on the grass verges and in other possibly illegal spots.

'Goodness!' she exclaimed. 'Where on earth are you going to park?'

'Never fear,' he said with a smile in his voice. 'I have that covered.' And he showed her a small red remote, which he then pointed slightly ahead of them.

Cleo stared as a large garage door on their right started to rise. It was one of two large garage doors separated by an elegant covered entranceway, behind which sat a two-storeyed home that was cement-rendered in a cream colour. Art deco in architecture, it had curved corners and large curved windows, the roof flat with a black trim. Before Cleo could observe anything further, Byron had driven into the garage, parking next to a small white hatchback.

'That's Gloria's car,' he said as he climbed out. 'She's the housekeeper. Mum and Lara keep their cars in the other garage. This spot is reserved for special visitors. Namely me,' he added with a boyish grin.

He strode around and opened the passenger door for her whilst she just sat there, stricken by a burst of nerves. She might look as if she was fit to be Byron's date for the night. But inside she still felt inadequate for the role. Inadequate for what he had in mind for her later tonight as well. As much as she wanted Byron—her mind spun every time she thought about being with him!—Cleo wasn't at all sure that he would find her…satisfactory.

She still found it hard to believe that he'd actually wanted her right back when they'd first met. But why would he lie? There was no reason for such a cruel deception. And he wasn't a cruel man. Cleo knew what a cruel man was like and Byron wasn't in that mould. He was, however, a very experienced lover who'd been to bed with lots of very beautiful and very confident women. His previous lovers would have known what to do to please a man. She'd never mastered that skill. According to Martin she'd always been too shy once she was naked. Too shy and too prudish. Never natural. Never passionate. And she probably *had* been like that. With him. But she didn't think she would be the same with Byron. Byron made her feel very sexy.

Cleo gulped and felt her nipples peak in her bra.

Don't think about that yet, she lectured herself as she undid her seat belt and took Byron's outstretched hand. *Think about this party first. Plus, meeting his mother.*

Now *that*, she wasn't looking forward to!

But as it turned out, meeting Rosalind Maddox wasn't anything like she'd been imagining. For starters, Byron's mother wasn't the overdressed face-lifted society matron that Cleo had been picturing. Okay, so she could pass for fifty instead of sixty at night, but there was no evidence of any nips and tucks around her face. On top of that, she didn't talk with a plum in her mouth and she was far from overdressed, wearing a silky lemon pant suit, which suited her ash-blonde hair. What surprised Cleo the most, however, was how warm and welcoming she was to her. Charming, in fact. Clearly, this was where Byron had learned his social skills.

'How lovely,' she said with seeming sincerity when she opened her card first. 'I do like cards with nice words in them. But I didn't expect anything else, Byron,' she added as she ripped off the wrapping paper. 'I thought the flowers were my present. Oh, thank you!' she gushed with genuine delight when she saw the book. 'Much better than last year's present, darling.'

'Mmm…' was all Byron said to that.

Rosalind smiled a rather mischievous smile. 'So!' she said, putting her book and card down on a side table. They were in a huge living room, which overlooked a tiled terrace, which itself overlooked the pool, and a tropical garden filled with fairy lights. Cleo could hear the sea beyond, washing gently against the sand. 'How long have you two been going out together?'

'Not long,' Byron replied.

'And how did you meet?'

'Cleo's Scott McAllister's PA. McAllister is a mining magnate. I've been thinking of investing in his company.'

His mother looked taken aback. 'Really? That's a bit unusual for you, Byron.'

Byron shrugged. 'What's life if you don't broaden your horizons occasionally?'

Rosalind looked from her son to Cleo, her intelligent blue eyes showing Cleo that she recognised she was different from Byron's usual choice of girlfriend. Though, of course, she wasn't a *real* girlfriend. Their relationship wasn't heading anywhere but bed. Which was fine by Cleo. That was all she wanted too.

Wasn't it?

'Now I'll have to go and mingle, my darlings,' Rosalind said, encompassing both of them with her words, and her smile. 'Why don't you do the same? There are lots of interesting people here.'

'Where's Lara?' Byron asked before his mother could escape. 'And Jasper?'

'Gone to one of her girlfriends' for the night. She said having to make chit-chat with my crowd would be sheer torture. And where Lara goes, Jasper is sure to follow. Now go get your lovely girl a glass of champagne. I bought the best.'

'Of course you did,' Byron muttered when his mother was out of earshot.

'What's with the sarcasm?' Cleo said straight away. 'I like your mother. She's sweet.'

'And she liked you. The reason she was so nice is that she's already planning our wedding in her head.'

'Don't be ridiculous!' Cleo exclaimed, shocked.

'She's very keen to see me married.'

'But not to me, surely!'

Byron frowned. 'Why not you?'

'I'm not your usual style of girlfriend. Even she saw that.'

'Maybe you're better.'

She hated that she flushed under his compliment. And for a split second imagined actually becoming Mrs Byron Maddox. She'd vowed at Martin's funeral never to put her life in a man's hands again, and she meant to keep that vow. Not that Byron would ever propose to someone like her, anyway.

'Let's not get carried away here, Byron,' she stated firmly. 'I only came with you tonight because you wanted protection from your mother's matchmaking agenda. And I only agreed to Grace making me over because it was time I did something about my appearance. For myself, not for you. *Or* for your mother. So please, don't let her think there's anything serious between us because that wouldn't be fair. To her or to me. Yes, I want to go to bed with you. Trust me when I say that's a rather shocking admission for me to make. But it begins and ends there.'

Byron could not believe how angry her speech made him. Why, he wasn't sure, because she was only telling him the truth, as she saw it.

His truth, however, was different. Each minute he spent with her made him want more. And he wasn't just referring to sex. Yes, he wanted to take her to bed. But he also wanted more than just a fling, or an affair, or whatever it was she seemed hell-bent on calling it. Maybe she didn't even want *that* much. It sure sounded like it.

'Are you saying you just want a one-night stand with me?' he demanded to know. 'Is that what you're saying?' He tried to contain his fury but it was impossible. Hot blood was bubbling along his veins and his hands were curled into fists at his side.

'No,' she replied hesitantly, her staring eyes blinking several times before adopting a rather cool expression. 'No, I don't think one night will be enough.'

Byron sucked in sharply, his body hardening, his heart squeezing tight at her unexpected but seriously exciting admission.

'It certainly won't be enough for me,' he growled, his eyes locking with hers until her mask of composure began to crumble.

He would have left his mother's party right then and there if they hadn't been collared by a couple of guests looking for fresh conversation. They were Rosalind's rather elderly next-door neighbours so Byron felt obliged to stay a while, so as not to be horribly rude. He introduced Cleo, who soon went quiet by his side, leaving it up to him to play the charming companion and witty conversationalist. Which, quite frankly, was not what he wanted to do, despite his being used to such a role. He was anxious to play a different role now, his mind already projecting ahead to that moment when he had Cleo naked in his bed and where he would seduce her utterly until she said yes to whatever he wanted. There would be no physical demand she would refuse. No emotional demand, either. If he wanted her to become his girlfriend for real, she would say yes. If he wanted her to become his secret mistress, she would say yes to that too. He would not countenance her spurning him, or deciding when enough was enough. *He* was going to decide that, damn it.

Never before had Byron experienced such ruthless urges in his pursuit of a woman. But then, he'd been rather ruthless from the start, hadn't he, doing things he didn't really want to do, just to be with her? And it was all her fault! Or her husband's fault, the one who'd fallen ill way too young then died on her, leaving her with a broken heart and an inability to fall in love again. She probably thought she was betraying the man she still loved by even wanting to be with another man. That was why she was trying to restrict herself to sex only, and only for a couple of nights.

But that was not how it was going to be. That was not what Byron wanted.

And, of course, what you want is all that matters, isn't it? Never mind her feelings. You just go for what you want and to hell with her broken heart!

Byron shut his eyes for a moment, at the same time telling that infernal voice to go jump.

'I heard your father is selling his house here in Sydney,' the neighbour said.

Byron tried to focus. 'Yes, that's right,' he agreed.

'Well, the market is right for selling property,' the man went on. 'But not so good for mining, little lady,' he directed at Cleo.

Byron whisked two glasses of champagne from a passing waiter and pressed one into Cleo's hands. 'Sorry, folks,' he said to the neighbours, 'but I need to speak to my mother about something. Great to see you again.' And he steered Cleo in the direction of his mother, who was out by the pool, chatting away to a male politician he despised and a female reality show host who had possibly been invited as one of the candidates for the role of his next fiancée. She beamed when she saw him approaching, her smile as over the top as the rest of her. Byron immediately did an about-face and shepherded Cleo into the kitchen where Gloria was helping the caterers.

'Hi there, Byron,' Gloria said warmly. 'So who have we got here?' she added, looking Cleo up and down.

Byron introduced Cleo before quietly telling Gloria that he wanted to escape.

'Mum won't notice I've gone for a while,' he said whilst downing some of the tasty-looking finger food sitting on the breakfast bar. 'Could you tell her when she finally notices my absence that Cleo felt a migraine coming on and I took her home? Say I didn't say goodbye personally because I was afraid I might get eaten by the cougar she was talking to at the time.'

Gloria laughed. 'There's a few of those in there.'

Byron smiled and put his arm around Cleo's shoulders. 'Want something to eat before we go, darling?'

She shook her head from side to side, her eyes wide, her shoulders trembling a little.

Her nerves moved him and pricked at his conscience. But not enough to change his mind.

'Okay, then finish up that champagne and we'll be off.'

CHAPTER FOURTEEN

'YOU SHOULDN'T HAVE called me darling,' Cleo said shakily as Byron backed out of the garage. 'Gloria will tell your mother and she'll jump to all the wrong conclusions.'

His sideways glance carried a hint of irritation. 'Does it really matter? We won't be coming back here any time soon.'

'Your mother might ring you and ask awkward questions.'

'Probably. But I can handle my mother, Cleo. It's *you* I'm finding hard to handle,' he ground out. 'Will you please just stop with the endless complications? I get that you don't want a real relationship with me. I get that you're way out of your comfort zone even agreeing to go to bed with me. But you have a right to a sex life, as do I. We're adults, Cleo. We don't have to answer to other people for what we do behind closed doors.'

Cleo winced at the exasperation in his voice. Or was it frustration she was hearing?

She herself was almost crippled with frustration. Plus a huge lump of fear. When Byron had swept her out of his mother's house, anxiety had set in her stomach like concrete before rising to lodge in her throat, making her voice raspy and her heart in danger of stopping. The rest of her body, however, had gone into overdrive, every nerve ending buzzing and burning with a need that was almost beyond belief.

Out of her comfort zone? More like out of this world!

'I… I'm sorry,' she choked out, though not at all sure what she was sorry for. Surely she had a right to make her feelings clear. She didn't like it when Byron rode roughshod over them.

Byron heaved a huge sigh. 'I'm sorry too. I shouldn't be snapping and snarling at you like this. It's not necessary. Or nice. I guess I'm somewhat frustrated. I haven't had sex since I broke up with Simone and I'm not at my best with celibacy.'

Did it please her that he hadn't had sex for over six weeks? His admission certainly surprised her.

The honesty of his statement actually pleased Cleo more than the content. Was she supposed to be impressed that he'd gone without sex for such a *long* time? she thought somewhat tartly.

Poor thing.

'I haven't had sex in over five years,' she told him bluntly before she could think better of it. 'Not since Martin was diagnosed with cancer.' Actually, she'd stopped having sex with him before that, having decided at long last to leave him. 'After he started on the chemo he wasn't interested.'

'I see,' Byron said in a rather cryptic tone before falling silent.

On Cleo's part, she couldn't think of anything to say, a perverse embarrassment joining her nervous tension, which actually heightened her desires.

'In that case,' he said after a minute or two, 'I don't think even two nights will be enough. I would suggest you put aside every night for the next week to spend with me. And possibly lunchtimes as well,' he added, slanting her a bad-boy smile.

'You wish,' she said, but she was smiling as well. How could she not? Byron could charm the pants off any woman.

'Only if *you* wish, my darling. I am at your disposal for as long as you want me.'

'You have to stop calling me darling.' It did terrible things to her. Silly, weakening things.

'Why?'

'You know why.'

'You're being difficult again. I can see you need a man with a firm hand.'

Cleo had to laugh. That was the last thing she needed. Or wanted.

Byron frowned. 'What did that laugh mean? It had a strange edge to it.'

'I'm a strange woman.'

'An enigmatic one, at least. Why *haven't* you had sex since your husband died? I mean, it's been three years, Cleo. Long enough for you to move on.'

Cleo wished she could tell him the total truth, but simply couldn't bring herself to be that disloyal to Martin. He hadn't been a bad man, just programmed badly by his father. Not that that was any excuse, really.

'Would you believe me if I said I haven't met a man—until you—who I wanted to have sex with?'

'As flattering as that idea is, no, I don't believe it.'

'It's true.'

'Really and truly?'

'Yes.'

'Wow.'

Byron wished he could believe her but he didn't. Not totally. There was some other reason, and he suspected it wasn't because she was still holding a torch for her dead husband. What kind of man wouldn't want the comfort of his wife's body when he was ill, or even dying? Surely that would be when he wanted it the most.

Maybe he was just ignorant of what chemo did to one's body, or insensitive to the man's feelings at the time, but he didn't buy her reason. Byron had had an inkling for some time that Cleo's marriage hadn't been perfectly happy; that her decision not to marry again came from bad memories, not good ones. A woman who'd been happy in marriage would surely have wanted to experience that happiness again. His father had been happy in his own first marriage for many years, which was why he'd wanted to try again. Byron himself wanted to marry because he believed marriage and a family would complete him. Making money was all very well, but it couldn't match the satisfaction and joy from a loving and committed relationship. And from children of your own.

If only, he thought as he glanced over at Cleo…

Don't start going there, Byron. She's not for you.

'I presume you're not on the pill, then,' he said as he sped towards the city through blessedly light traffic.

'No.'

'No sweat. I always use protection anyway. Men like me don't take chances.'

'What do you mean?'

She sounded genuinely perplexed, which was another reason why he liked her so much. Despite her demanding and challenging job, Cleo wasn't worldly. In some ways, she was an innocent. He wouldn't mind betting she'd been a virgin on her wedding night. Or at least until she was engaged.

'Rich men are targets for gold-diggers,' he told her bluntly. 'A pregnancy is the best way to trap a rich man into marriage. Or at least get a regular income for life. Even when I was engaged I continued to use condoms.'

'That's a sad way to have to live,' Cleo said quietly.

Byron shrugged. 'No point in being naive.'

'I suppose not…'

'I've been engaged twice, actually,' he admitted.

'I know. I looked you up on the Internet before I met you that first day.'

He laughed. 'I looked up McAllister. But *you* weren't mentioned.'

'I wouldn't have been,' she said before turning her head to gaze out of the passenger window. After a while, she turned back to face him. 'There's something else I feel I should tell you, Byron,' she went on with a hint of worry in her voice.

'What?'

'I had a security check done on you before we went to Townsville together. I hope you're not offended.'

'Not at all. I wouldn't expect anything less of a smart PA. Did you find out anything worth knowing?'

'Not much more than I already knew. You were captain of your school. And very good at sport. And you dated lots of stunningly beautiful girls whilst you worked for your father in America.'

'True. I've been known to be shallow where the opposite sex is concerned. Not to mention stupid. I'm sure Grace told you as much on Friday.'

'Grace never said a single derogatory word about you.'

'That's good to know. Look, it's great having a chat. Normally, it passes the time pleasantly during a drive, but to be honest I don't want to talk right now. I want to concentrate on getting you home to my place as fast as possible. Frankly, I'm finding it hard to think of anything but how I'm the first man you've wanted to have sex with for five flaming years. If anything is designed to make me a blithering idiot, it's that thought, believe me, so, if you don't mind, could you please shut that gorgeous mouth of yours till I have a much better use for it?'

CHAPTER FIFTEEN

CLEO'S LIPS PRESSED firmly shut whilst her mind filled with the various uses Byron might have for her mouth. There was kissing, of course, but she suspected he meant something else, that other oral activity that she'd never fancied before yet which suddenly seemed, oh, so exciting.

Her face flamed as she imagined how it would feel to do that to him. And more. She longed to run her lips over every inch of his magnificent male body, to learn what pleased him most, to make him stiffen with desire. For *her*, not those other women he'd dated or been engaged to. For ordinary old Cleo, who'd rarely made a man's head turn in her life.

But she was not ordinary old Cleo tonight. She was beautiful and sexy and ready to be everything any man could want, even one as experienced as Byron. She would be bold and adventurous and imaginative. She would be wildly passionate and without inhibition. She would be wicked.

Suddenly, Cleo couldn't get enough breath into her body. Her chest tightened as her heart slammed against her ribs and her nostrils flared. She had to open her mouth and suck in some life-giving air. *Had* to!

'You all right?' Byron immediately asked her, his head swivelling around.

'I'm not allowed to talk,' she threw back at him through panting lips.

'We're almost there,' he growled.

Cleo blinked as her dazed eyes cleared to take in her surrounds. She hadn't noticed them crossing the bridge or entering the city streets. She'd been off in that darkly erotic world that he'd created with his earlier words, weaving fantasies in her head that demanded all of her concentration to create. Because she wasn't working on memory. Just imagination.

Within minutes they were parked in a subterranean car park and Byron was bundling her out of the passenger seat and into his arms.

'I can't wait,' he ground out, and his mouth crashed down on hers.

But as quickly as his lips had descended, they shot upwards, Byron's handsome face twisting with total frustration.

'Damn and blast,' he swore. 'I can't do it here. I can't do that to you. Not after five years. Come on.' And grabbing her empty hands—her purse was still in the car— he pulled her in the direction of the lift well, which had a sign saying private above it.

CHAPTER SIXTEEN

'I... I THINK I'm having a panic attack,' Cleo choked out as the lift zoomed up to the top floor. Her heart was going like the clappers and she was finding it difficult to breathe.

'Poor darling,' Byron said, and pulled her close. 'But I doubt it's a genuine panic attack. You're just overexcited. I'm somewhat excited myself.'

Cleo groaned, then turned to press her flushed face into his chest. 'You are going to be *so* disappointed in me,' she said, her voice muffled.

As the lift purred to a halt Byron eased her away from his chest and cupped her heated cheeks with his own rather warm hands. 'Now don't be silly,' he said firmly. 'Disappointment is going to be the *last* emotion I feel when I make love to you.'

Cleo sighed, thrilled that he'd said *make love* rather than *have sex*. Her crisis of confidence, however, hadn't entirely abated. So much for her resolve to be bold, and imaginative, and adventurous. Byron was right. She was a silly woman. *Very* silly.

When he took her hand to lead her from the lift she

pulled back, afraid suddenly that she was making a big mistake. As much as she'd liked his romantic words, she didn't really want Byron to *make love* to her, did she? Because if he did that, she might fall in love with him, and what would be the good of that? There was no use kidding herself into thinking he would ever love her in return. She also didn't want to start secretly dreaming that Byron might consider her one day for the role of his wife, and the mother of his children. Such dreams could only lead to heartbreak. And she'd had enough heartbreak in her life already, thank you very much. Not that she *wanted* to get married again. But if ever there was a man who might persuade her otherwise, it was Byron.

Byron rolled his eyes at her. 'What's the matter *now*?' he growled. 'If you tell me you've changed your mind, then I'm going to take a running jump off my terrace. And might I remind you that it's forty floors down.'

Cleo sucked in a deep, gathering breath, determined to be sensible and not silly.

'I haven't changed my mind,' she said with as much cool as she could muster in the face of her about-to-combust body. 'I just don't want *any* emotion to be involved with what we do tonight. I want to keep things strictly...physical.'

Byron felt like strangling her. Was there no pleasing this woman? Talk about contrary.

'Right,' he bit out. He supposed he could do that. He'd been doing it most of his life. But it wasn't the way he wanted to play things tonight.

Angry now, he bent to sweep her up into his arms and carried her through the open lift doors. 'Is this physical enough for you?' he ground out.

'Please put me down,' she told him sternly when he stopped by his locked front door.

'Only if you promise to stop inventing reasons not to do this. You want it as much as I do, Cleo, and I don't appreciate you playing word games with me.'

Her dark eyes registered real distress. 'But I would *never* do that. I just wanted to be honest.'

'Honest, Cleo? Well, take this for honesty. I'll be as emotional as I like when I make love to you tonight. This is not a one-night stand. How many times do I have to tell you? I like you a lot and want to be with you. If I wanted just physical, there are women who will give me that. Some don't even charge. But I don't want that from you, Cleo. I want *more* than that.'

'Oh,' she said, tears filling her eyes.

Which put paid to her ridiculous request to keep emotion out of tonight, Byron thought with a mixture of relief and guilt. He'd been harsh with her just now, he realised, possibly because he'd been jealous, thinking *she* might have been thinking of her dead husband when she asked him to keep things strictly sexual.

'Please don't cry,' he said, his voice still slightly exasperated. Though more with himself, than her. It worried him that his emotions might already be getting out of hand with this woman. He didn't *want* to fall in love with her. There was obviously no future in that. 'There's no reason to cry,' he added, and hugged her close. His heart immediately squeezed tight and he wondered if his hormones were tricking him again. Because they were running at full force tonight, had been ever since she'd opened the door to him and he'd seen how beautiful she could look. It annoyed him that he couldn't be sure of his own feelings any more. But that wasn't anything new, was it? All he could be sure of at this moment was how much he wanted to have sex with Cleo.

He lowered her back onto her feet, then fished out his keys.

Cleo did her best to get herself together whilst Byron opened his front door.

He was right. There was no reason to cry. And yes, she did want this as much—maybe *more*—than he did. But she was still very nervous. She hadn't been naked in front of any man except Martin. Just thinking about that inevitability was adding nerves to an already heightened situation.

Cleo swallowed. She wasn't ashamed of her body. In actual fact, she thought it was pretty good. But she'd seen the photos online of the two women Byron had been engaged to. They hadn't just been pretty good. Their bodies had been spectacular!

'You're doing it again,' Byron said, and glared at her.

'Doing what?'

'Trying to come up with some reason to back out.'

'No, I'm not,' she denied, her chin lifting even whilst she quaked inside.

'Good.' He threw open the door and waved her inside. 'Take the first hallway on your left and go right to the very end. The double doors there lead into the master bedroom. I'll be right behind you once I deadlock this door.'

Cleo strode into the spacious foyer with her head held high and her courage a few footsteps behind. She didn't stop to look around before she turned left down a wide tiled hallway, though a quick glimpse ahead showed a living area that was bigger than her whole house. On reaching the double doors, she opened one and stepped into the master bedroom.

Oh, my, she thought as she glanced around.

The room was ginormous, with a king-size bed and a large television on the wall opposite the foot of the bed. There was also a separate sitting area with a small bar in a nearby corner. Behind the very comfy-looking sofa were French doors leading out onto a wide terrace, beyond which she could see the lights of the city. The furniture was elegant and mostly white, with frosted glass on the table tops. The walls and ceilings were white, the carpet a dark grey. The designer—and there had to have been one—had used red as an accent colour. The sofa was red crushed velvet and the two armchairs were made in a red and white striped linen. One white cane chair sat in each corner on either side of the bed, which had a grey and white striped duvet, along with a mountain of white pillows. A grey fake fur throw was draped across the foot of the bed. The bedside lamps were chrome, with simple but elegant white shades. There were no curtains on the windows that framed the French doors, just white plantation shutters.

'You like?' Byron murmured as he materialised behind her, his hands resting on her shoulders.

Cleo would have shrugged if she could have. 'What's not to like?' she said. 'It's a beautiful room.'

'Which I hope you're going to become very familiar with,' he said, and turned her around to face him.

CHAPTER SEVENTEEN

BYRON LOCKED EYES with Cleo, fearful that she might turn tail and run. There was no doubting that there was still worry in her eyes.

No more talk, he decided. It was time for action!

So he kissed her. Not the rather savage, wildly passionate kiss he'd given her down in the car park. A softer, slower, more reassuring kiss, which told her she had nothing to fear from being here with him. When her mouth flowered open under his and a low moan escaped her lungs, he knew she was his. At least for now.

The pressure of his mouth immediately increased, his tongue darting forward to dance with hers, his own body struggling to contain the fire that had been on a slow burn for her since the day they'd met. The temptation to rush things was acute, but he resisted. He didn't want to frighten her. He wanted to take things slowly. But, damn, it was hard. *He* was hard. Harder than he'd ever been.

Was that groan his? Or hers?

Possibly it came from both of them.

Suddenly, all bets were off. And so were his good intentions.

His head lifted and he stared down at her. Her eyes were shut and she was breathing fast. Finally, she opened her eyes and looked up into his. Then she did the most wonderful thing. She smiled.

'You're a very good kisser,' she said.

'And you're a very good kiss*ee*.'

Cleo laughed. 'Is there such a word?'

'There is now. But no more talk, Cleo. Seriously. I told myself that I would be patient. That I would show you the best time in the world. And I will. The second time around. And definitely the third. But just right at this moment, all I can think about is being inside you. So if you don't mind, I would like to undress you. And quickly. Please don't stop me.'

Stop him! The thought never crossed her mind. It was way too full of images that his hot promises had evoked.

He undressed her with a speed that smacked of a lot of experience undressing women. Not that Cleo cared about that. Not right at that moment, anyway. Within seconds she was down to her underwear and shoes, her lovely blue outfit tossed aside as if it hadn't cost her a small fortune. But she didn't care about that, either. All she cared about was the hunger in his eyes, and the hunger in her own body. God, but she wanted him inside her too!

'What delicious breasts you have, Cleo,' he murmured after he removed her bra and tossed it aside also. 'Full and soft and natural.' His hands cupped and lifted them, his mouth bending to nuzzle into the cleavage he'd made. 'I'm going to enjoy these. Kick off those lethal shoes you're wearing and lie down. But don't take off those sexy satin panties. I want to do that myself.'

Byron undressed himself in front of her, piece by piece. His body was muscled, with a flat stomach and impressive abs and the kind of chest that you often saw on male models. No hair for starters, and taut pink nipples sitting in the middle of well-defined pecs.

Cleo's head whirled at how much she wanted to kiss them. And lick them. And suck them. She wanted to do the same to the rest of him as well. She wanted… Oh, she wanted so much!

'Keep looking at me like that, Cleo,' Byron growled as he joined her on the bed, 'and I might not last long enough to get inside you.'

Her dark eyes widened.

'Hell, but you are one gorgeous woman. I love this look,' he said, and ran his hands over her hairless sex, Cleo having submitted to a rather ruthless waxing earlier today at the beauty salon. A full Hollywood, the girl had called it.

'Oh…' she moaned when one of his fingers made a more intimate exploration.

'Wow,' he said, and glanced up at her. 'You're as impatient as I am.'

She nodded, her tongue thick in her throat.

His first thrust literally took her breath away. How amazing he felt. How…big!

He filled her completely. And yet she wanted him in deeper. Her legs lifted to wrap high around his back, her hands clasping his bottom, her nails digging in as she pulled him further into her. He groaned, then swore.

'Hell, Cleo,' he went on raggedly. 'Give me a break, will you?'

'Just shut up and move,' she threw at him, beside herself with the most excruciating need. She'd never experienced an urge so powerful. Now that he was inside her, she simply could not wait. She needed to come, and she needed it *now*!

As he thrust harder and faster, Cleo could feel herself getting closer, finally climaxing in a burst of pleasure that left her moaning with a mixture of wild abandon and the fiercest embarrassment. How could she have spoken to him like that? Oh, God, he was still moving. And everything started twisting inside her again. Hot air shot out of her lungs as her lips gasped wide. She was going to come again. She was sure of it. But then he came, and she came with him, their loud cries of mutual release echoing off the walls.

Finally, they both fell silent, Byron collapsing across her, his weight pushing her into the soft mattress. When she made some sound in protest, he swore, then rolled off her, the suddenness of his withdrawal bringing another sound to her lips.

'Sorry,' he muttered.

Cleo didn't want his apology. She was beyond wanting anything. All the wanting that had built up in her since meeting Byron had just been thoroughly quenched. She was no longer on fire. She was nothing but ash. Her legs were lifeless, her hands flopped to her sides, her body a dead weight on the bed. Her eyes closed on a long sigh. Sleep was just a heartbeat away. She vaguely heard him sigh as well, after which she heard him sit up. But then she heard nothing.

* * *

Byron stood next to the bed for a long moment, staring down at her unconscious body.

Various emotions warred for supremacy in his feelings.

Dismay. She just wanted him for the sex after all.

Disappointment. He had honestly expected more from her than that.

But finally, once he got over the huge blow to his ego, came determination. He wasn't going to let her get away, was he? He wanted more from her than a few miserable nights. And he aimed to have her, for as long as they still desired each other. Which he suspected could be quite some time. There was no doubt that the sexual chemistry between them was very strong. Stronger than it had been with either Simone or Eva.

But sexual chemistry was not necessarily love. True love, Byron accepted, was something he'd not yet experienced. It would be foolish of him to start thinking he was in love with Cleo, just because he liked her a lot. And desired her like crazy. Maybe, in time, he would know for sure what his true feelings for her were. But right now, his confidence in his ability to read his feelings had been rocked by his two broken engagements. After all, he'd thought he'd been in love on both those occasions. And he'd been dead wrong then, hadn't he?

Only his lust for Cleo was crystal-clear, as hers was for him. Byron took some comfort from that, deciding that he would use that lust to keep her in his life, and in his bed. Then hopefully, in time, all would sort itself out. Meanwhile, he would make her see that she didn't have to shy away from a proper relationship with him, just because she believed she should stay loyal to her dead husband.

If that *was* the reason. Byron still wasn't entirely convinced that her marriage had been all that perfect. Hopefully, he could get her to talk about it at some stage. Women usually liked to tell him everything about their past lives. Not so Cleo, it seemed. Maybe when McAllister got back from his second honeymoon, he could find out more about Cleo from him. Or maybe he could subtly question Doreen when he dropped by to take Cleo out. Though that might prove awkward, given she was the mother of Cleo's dead husband. No, that wasn't going to work.

Hell on earth! Byron's hands lifted to run through his hair. It really bothered him how unsure he was about his feelings for this woman. Being unsure about anything went against his basic nature.

Cleo slept on, oblivious of his angst. She wasn't being torn apart by ongoing frustrations, was she? She was one thoroughly satisfied woman.

Well, I'm not bloody well satisfied. Not even remotely!

Scowling, Byron picked up the rug that lay across the foot of the bed, throwing it over Cleo's naked body before whirling and marching into the bathroom where he would have a long, hot, soothing shower, after which he would calm himself down with some food and a drink. Then, once he had his temper firmly under control, he would return and wake Cleo up. Because he wasn't finished with her for tonight. He had more work to do, slaking his own rapidly recovering desire, as well as showing her that she couldn't go back to her sexless life; that she needed a more permanent lover who could make her body burn with desire.

CHAPTER EIGHTEEN

CLEO WOKE TO the most delicious sensation. It took her a few seconds to realise what it was. And *where* she was.

Her first reaction was a hot jab of humiliation. Had she really said that to him?

Just shut up and move!

Yes, Cleo. You really said it. And he did move. And you came, not once, but twice. And yes, it felt fantastic.

Byron's fingertip running up and down her spine at this moment felt pretty incredible, too.

A low moan was wrenched from her throat.

'You're awake,' he murmured, his breath warm against her ear.

When she went to roll over, he pushed her back. 'Let's try it this way, shall we?' he suggested, oh, so smoothly.

Before she could protest, he'd teased her into a pool of molten desire, and then eased into her from behind, his hands coming round to cup her breasts, the pads of his thumbs rubbing over her nipples till they grew hard and so sensitive that she could not keep silent.

'You are so sexy,' he crooned as he rocked back and forth inside her. 'I don't know how you could have gone so long without this.'

Because I've never had *this,* she could have told him. But she didn't. She kept silent on the subject and just wallowed in amazement at the glorious sensations rocketing through her. Soon, she just had to move too, lifting her bottom and pressing herself back against him. He groaned, then picked up his rhythm, both in power and depth. His hands tightened on her breasts when she matched him thrust for thrust, their mating turning from tender to tempestuous.

'Oh, God,' she choked out. Because it quickly became too much. The electric pleasure. The crippling tension. The bittersweet knowledge that Byron would only ever be her lover. And a temporary one at that. It would be naive of her to wish for more.

If only Byron weren't who he was, she started thinking. If only he were an ordinary man, with an ordinary job and an ordinary life. But then, an ordinary man would not have infatuated her nearly as much. Or turned her on like this. Or made her yearn for what could never be.

His climax triggered her own, their bodies shuddering together as they found release. But as he held her close and whispered sweet nothings into her ear, a huge wave of dismay swamped Cleo, dampening any lingering pleasure over what had been another incredible orgasm.

I can't keep doing this, came the agonised lecture to herself. *It will soon become sheer torture!*

But at the same time Cleo knew she could not stop. Not whilst he wanted her, despite the fact that his wanting her would not last. Men like Byron didn't stay with girls like Cleo. This was just an aberration from his normal life. A fling. She'd been a challenge to him at first. Something different. But she wasn't a challenge any longer, was she? She was here, in his bed, accommodating his wishes without a word of protest. Seemingly without a will of her own.

She hated that last thought. If there was one thing Cleo prided herself on these days, it was that she was her own person. Totally independent, with a mind of her own and a willpower and character to match. Or so she'd imagined, until she met Byron. When she was with him, her willpower quickly grew weak, and her so-called character became decidedly lacking.

It came to her that he would grow bored with her even more quickly if she became a yes girl. And she didn't want him to grow bored with her. Not yet.

'I think,' she said into the silence of the room, 'that I should go home now.'

He laughed. He actually laughed. 'Not quite yet, my darling,' he said, the endearment making her wince. Because she wasn't his darling. Not really. 'Cinderella doesn't go home until after midnight. And it's only just past eleven.'

She gasped when he withdrew abruptly, then again when he scooped her up into his arms.

'If I recall rightly, I said three times, not two,' he said with a wicked twinkle in his eyes as he carried her into the hugest bathroom she'd ever seen.

Somehow, she found her tongue as he lowered her onto the marble-tiled floor.

'You really are a naughty boy, aren't you?' she said, determined not to be wishy-washy or blindly besotted.

If she was going to do this, then she wasn't about to fall into the same submissive role she'd played with Martin.

His lopsided smile was very sexy. 'I'm hardly a boy. But I will confess to some naughtiness on occasion.'

'Please don't assume that I will say yes to everything you want,' she told him firmly, an ironic statement considering she was standing, stark naked, before him.

Still, she liked the admiring light that glittered in his beautiful blue eyes. 'I would never assume anything where you are concerned, Cleo. Now, could we get back to business?'

Her eyebrows arched. '*Business*, Byron?'

'It's just a figure of speech. Don't take offence.'

'I'll try not to.'

He frowned. 'You can be very difficult when you want to be, can't you?'

'Yes,' she agreed. 'So be warned.'

His frown changed into a disarming smile. 'Consider me warned. So, do you want to have a shower with me, or not?'

Silly question.

'I suppose I might suffer through it.'

His eyes narrowed until he realised she was being sarcastic.

'You are a naughty girl sometimes, aren't you?'

'I'm hardly a girl,' she said, echoing his earlier riposte. 'And until I met you, I was never ever naughty.'

'Thank goodness you met me, then, sweetheart. Because if that's the case, you were in danger of becoming boring.'

She speared him with a droll look. 'There are worse things in life than boring.'

* * *

Byron heard the bitter note in her voice and wondered what she was referring to.

But he didn't wonder for long. Impossible to think much once she wound seductive arms up around his neck and pulled his head down onto hers.

CHAPTER NINETEEN

CLEO SLEPT IN the next morning for the first time in years. She could not believe it when she picked up her phone from her bedside table and saw that it was nearly noon.

Not wanting to dwell on the reasons behind her blissful exhaustion, she sat up abruptly then swung her feet onto the rug beside her bed. Shaking her head lest she start thinking and worrying, Cleo shoved her feet into her pink slippers, levered herself upright, drew on her cosy pink dressing gown then made her way with feigned bravado out to face her mother-in-law.

Doreen was in the kitchen, making coffee. Mungo was sprawled on the tiles nearby, but he rose when Cleo made an appearance in the doorway, limping over to her with his big brown tail wagging happily but his dark eyes as doleful as ever.

'And how are you this morning, big boy?' she said as she gave him a scratch behind his ears. Doreen immediately swung around from where she'd been facing the electric kettle, her eyes registering immediate curiosity.

Cleo suppressed a sigh. She wasn't looking forward

to answering Doreen's questions. And there would be questions. Lots of them.

To lie or not to lie. That was *Cleo's* question.

'Coffee?' Doreen offered.

'Please.'

Cleo pulled out a chair and sat down, this time forgetting to hide her sigh.

'You sound tired,' Doreen said as she carried two mugs over to the table.

'I guess I'm not used to being a social butterfly,' was Cleo's misleading answer.

'You must have had a good time to stay out so late. And no, I wasn't deliberately spying. You know I have to get up at least once a night to go to the toilet. But yes, I did look out of the front window and yes, I saw Byron Maddox kiss you goodnight.'

Oh-oh, Cleo thought ruefully.

'It…um…didn't look like a platonic goodnight peck,' Doreen added.

Oh, dear. No lying, then. It would only make things worse.

She decided it was best to be totally honest—up to a point—especially considering Byron had asked her out to dinner tonight, and she'd already said yes.

'He's very nice,' she said, somewhat defensively.

'I agree. I liked him enormously. More than I thought I would. I already knew *you* liked him but I imagined a man of his wealth would be too arrogant. Yet he isn't. I should have trusted your judgment. You wouldn't have liked any man these days who wasn't genuinely nice.'

Cleo heard the secret message behind Doreen's words.

Of course, she must have known what Martin had been like. Like father, like son. But they'd never discussed his failings as a husband. Not whilst he'd been alive. And certainly not now that he was dead.

'But what about his mother?' Doreen asked. 'Was *she* nice to you?'

'Very nice. I was surprised, I can tell you.'

'You shouldn't have been surprised. You looked utterly gorgeous. Clearly, your makeover made Byron Maddox stand up and take notice too. I'll bet he asked you out again, didn't he?'

'He did, actually,' Cleo said, doing her best to sound nonchalant as she picked up her coffee for a sip. She took it black so it was still very hot.

'When?'

'Tonight. For dinner.' But she knew they wouldn't be lingering over a five-course meal. He'd have her back at that corrupting penthouse of his like a shot.

Cleo's mouth dried as she thought of all they had done in the shower last night, then afterwards, back in bed, where she'd been bolder than she had ever imagined being with a man!

Cleo didn't regret any of it. What she regretted this morning was her inability to prevent herself from becoming totally bewitched by the man. Of course, her claim that she only wanted a strictly sexual relationship was a bald-faced lie. Any normal woman would want more from Byron than that. She was just protecting herself from future heartbreak by covering up her feelings inside a false shell.

Impossible to blame herself for that. But it was a pity

that she had to lie, to pretend. If only she'd been of a different ilk. One of those cold-blooded creatures who could use a man for sex and not care a whit for him. But she wasn't like that. Underneath her cool, sometimes distant façade lay a very responsive heart. It sang when she was with him. Quivered when he was inside her. Thudded when her mouth made love to him.

Still, she did find some personal satisfaction in having taken a firm stand over what she wanted, even if it encompassed a little white lie. She'd come a long way since Martin's death and wasn't about to allow herself to fall victim to another dominating man. And Byron was dominating. Not in the same way Martin was—there was no cruelty in Byron. But Cleo had no doubt that he liked everything his way.

'He's very good-looking, isn't he?' Doreen mused as she sipped her coffee.

Cleo nodded. That was putting it mildly. Byron was *exceptionally* good-looking.

'They say clothes maketh the man,' Doreen went on, 'but I suspect Byron would look just as good in his birthday suit.'

Cleo coughed, trying to sound very casual but somehow failing.

Doreen shot her a narrow-eyed glance.

'As much as I like to see you dating, Cleo, I wouldn't want you to start thinking Byron Maddox is looking for anything serious with you. Men like that end up with supermodels and socialites, not working-class girls.'

'I do know that, Doreen,' Cleo bit out. It was one thing to privately admit that this was true. Quite another to hear someone else say it. Because it made it more real. And more painful to acknowledge.

'You will be careful, won't you, dear? I'd hate to see you hurt. Have some fun with the man but don't take him seriously.'

Their landline phone rang and Doreen rose to collect the receiver off the kitchen wall.

'Hello,' she said as she carried it back to the table with her.

Her face lit up before she'd sat down. 'That's very sweet of you, Harvey,' she gushed.

Cleo's eyebrows arched and Doreen actually blushed. Good heavens! What was going on here? Harvey was a lot of things but not sweet. As for Doreen, she was definitely not a gusher. Or a blusher.

'No, no, it'll just be me and Mungo tonight,' Doreen informed her surprising caller. 'Cleo's going out. With Byron Maddox,' she added before Cleo could warn her not to say anything. She wished she could hear Harvey's reaction.

'Whatever you choose will be fine by me,' Doreen went on. 'I'm not fussy where food is concerned. As for the wine, I do prefer white. But not too dry.'

After another minute or so of slightly flirtatious conversation, Doreen said goodbye and hung up.

Cleo sent her a questioning look over the rim of the coffee mug.

'Harvey's bringing Chinese over tonight,' Doreen said, looking both delighted and somewhat sheepish. 'He wanted to see how Mungo was doing. He adores dogs, you see, and was worried about him.'

Cleo smothered a laugh. 'You honestly believe that's why he's coming?'

Doreen's kind face did its best to look haughty but failed dismally. 'That's what he said.'

Cleo had to smile. 'If Harvey adored dogs he wouldn't live in a high-rise apartment which doesn't allow pets. He can afford to buy a house, with the salary Scott pays him. A house with a yard. A yard which would accommodate even the biggest dog. The man is coming to see you, Doreen, not Mungo.' The dog's head lifted to the sound of his name, then lowered to the tiles again. 'Harvey obviously fancies you,' Cleo finished up.

'Oh,' Doreen said, looking delighted again.

Cleo shook her head then stood up to go have her shower. Life, she thought, was truly weird. Weird but also wonderful at times. Who would have imagined that Harvey would be smitten by Doreen? Not that she wasn't an attractive woman still. And yes, Harvey did have a certain macho appeal. It was funny how things worked out sometimes, she thought.

Cleo lifted her face into the warm stream of the shower and smoothed her hair back from her head. *He'd* done that to her last night. Smoothed her hair back from her head and held it tight so it couldn't fall across her face and hide what she was doing.

Her stomach clenched down hard at the decadent image of her kneeling before him in that shower.

He hadn't let her go all the way. Not then. But he hadn't stopped her later, when they were stretched out on top of the bed and she had access to his whole body. Oh, how she'd loved hearing the sounds he made as she made love to him. With her hands first, and then her mouth. Cleo still could not believe how much she'd enjoyed doing that. There'd been no sense of distaste, let alone disgust. Nothing but the joy of pleasing him, and the heady sense of power that came from listening to him losing control.

But was this really love? she asked herself. Or just infatuation, accompanied by her libido gone mad? She'd read that women peaked sexually in their thirties.

Well, she was coming up for thirty...

Her eyes closed against the confusion that threatened to overwhelm her. She'd been so sure last night that she was in love with Byron. But did she really know what being in love felt like? All she knew was that her feelings for Byron were different from what she'd felt for her husband. Of course, she'd believed herself madly in love with Martin when she agreed to marry him, but she knew now that her feelings back then had been a mirage. She'd been in love with being loved. And yes, Martin had been very good—initially—at making her feel loved. He'd been very good at making her feel good all round at first, his flattery and his compliments never-ending. But once their honeymoon was over and he had her firmly under his thumb with her family all gone and her life totally in his hands, he'd changed. Suddenly, their lives together had been reduced to endless restrictions and rules. Compliments had given way to criticisms, flattery to the finding of, oh, so many flaws.

'Don't you know how to make a bed at least?' she recalled him throwing at her one morning not long after

they were married. *'You're no damn good in it so you can at least learn how to make it.'*

After which he'd proceeded to show her how to do hospital corners. And Lord help her if she didn't follow his instructions exactly.

In the beginning, she'd tried to please him, determined to be a good wife. But in the end, she'd realised that it was impossible to please Martin.

At least Byron wasn't impossible to please…

She'd pleased him last night and she aimed to please him again tonight.

Don't think about love, Cleo, she told herself sternly as she snapped off the taps and stepped out of the shower. *Think of making love. And of making Byron lose control again.*

It was a heady thought, one that she hugged to herself for the rest of the day.

CHAPTER TWENTY

BYRON PULLED IN to Cleo's street right on seven, pleased to find a parking spot again. He backed into the angular space, turned off the engine and just sat there, being early in his eagerness to see Cleo again.

He'd rung her earlier in the afternoon, unable to go a whole day without at least hearing her voice.

You've got it bad, man, Jack would have said. Jack was his best friend when he'd lived in America. But they'd lost touch after Byron came back to Australia. Not a real friend, then, Byron acknowledged. He didn't have many real friends. Just acquaintances and business associates. He'd had heaps of friends at school and university but had left all of them behind when he'd left the country.

There again, seriously rich men found it hard to find real friends, Byron conceded. People who genuinely cared about you and not because of what you could do for them. The same problem arose with finding the right woman to marry.

Cleo couldn't be that right woman, could she? It was a sobering thought. After denying it to himself for so long, he began to wonder if she was perhaps exactly what he'd been looking for. The problem was, he couldn't trust himself—after all, he'd thought the same about Eva and Simone and then just as quickly realised it hadn't been real love, just infatuation. How would he ever know for sure?

As his father had advised, Cleo had a career of her own, and she certainly didn't have a gold-digging bone in her body. He also liked her a lot. Liked her intelligence and her honesty and, yes, her lack of worldliness.

Unfortunately, Byron wasn't sure if he was actually in love with her, which was a worry. He was damned sure, however, that *she* wasn't in love with *him*. Not to mention the fact that she didn't want to get married again, either.

Two rather huge hurdles, ones which Byron had no control over. He didn't like that. He didn't like it at all.

Feeling both exasperated and frustrated, he climbed out from behind the wheel and made his way down the side path of the narrow wooden house. A strange knot of nerves gathered in his stomach as his hand lifted to press the doorbell. The ring echoed through the house, followed by a deep woof from Mungo.

The dog stood guard next to Cleo when she opened the door, eyeing Byron with his usual wariness.

Cleo didn't look wary, however. She looked wickedly sexy. When he'd spoken to her earlier on the phone she'd asked what kind of restaurant he was taking her to so that she knew how to dress. He'd told her to dress casually, and in sensible shoes, since he intended to take the car back to his place first then walk down to a small Asian restaurant he often frequented, which had a casual ambience and served delicious food very quickly.

She'd laughed at that and said *good thinking* in a knowing tone, which had given him an instant erection, and which was still there, hiding beneath the brown suede jacket he was wearing over his favourite fawn chinos.

Nothing much was hidden with Cleo's outfit, however. The jeans she was wearing were not the awful ones she'd worn the other day. These were black and tight and expensive-looking, teamed with black ankle boots and a low-cut black silk top over which she sported a soft, red leather, crew-necked jacket, which only just reached her waist and which had a zipper instead of a lapel or buttons. Not done up. Just hanging loose, possibly so that he could smell the exotic perfume wafting from her sexily dressed body. Her hair was up, but in one of those loose just-got-out-of-her-lover's-bed styles. Her face wasn't overly made up, but her eyelids had a smoky look and her lips were glossed in the same colour as her jacket. Blood red.

Byron's own blood boiled as his eyes raked over her.

'Love the rock-chick outfit,' he said, and her eyes immediately widened.

'I was aiming for casual, like you said.'

'Sweetheart, there's nothing casual about the way you look tonight. Hope you're ready to eat quickly.'

The answering glitter in her eyes hit him below the belt with more force than a physical blow. Lust, not love, he decided ruefully, was still his priority here. Hers, too. It was a perversely disappointing realisation. His body, however, wasn't listening to his emotions. It was already on the burn.

'I've always been a quick eater,' she murmured, then more loudly, 'Ah, here's Harvey come to keep Doreen and Mungo company for the evening. Hi there, Harvey. Come and meet Byron.'

'Are you sure that Harvey chap's not a bikie?'

Cleo glanced up from where she was happily running her hands over Byron's naked body. They'd already made love once. And had another highly erotic shower after which they'd retired to bed for another round.

'No. He's not even an *ex*-bikie. But he does like motorcycles. And he is an ex-cop.'

'And he's your head of security?'

'Yes.'

'So, he already knows everything about me.'

'Everything that's on public record. Yes. But he doesn't know *this* about you,' she murmured, and replaced her hands with her mouth.

Cleo didn't want to talk about Harvey. Frankly, she didn't want to talk at all, having vowed to concentrate on sex from now on and not on other potentially distressing emotions. Which, in her opinion, should suit Byron. After all, he didn't want for ever. She was just a fling, a diversion, until a suitable bride came along.

Byron saw the distress in her eyes, and didn't know whether he was the cause. But she could be frustratingly distant at times, as if she was deliberately keeping her feelings hidden from him. Her eyes, however, often revealed things that gave him hope. He was sure he'd glimpsed real emotion there when he was inside her, face to face. He loved seeing that. He didn't love it when she focused on his body as if he were just a piece of meat. Yes, he enjoyed it when she went down on him. Hell, how could he not? She was very good at it. Nevertheless, the thought pained him where she'd learned her techniques. It seemed crazy to be jealous of a dead man. But he was. Clearly, he'd been wrong when he'd imagined their marriage hadn't been all that perfect. It must have been pretty good in the bedroom, at least.

How she'd gone so long without was a mystery. Unless you accepted the unpalatable truth that her grief over her husband's death was so great that she simply hadn't been able to bear being with another man for years and years.

Byron didn't want to accept that reality, but it seemed illogical to keep denying the facts that were staring him in the face. *She* was staring him in the face, her eyes offended and unhappy.

'You're so beautiful,' he said, cupping her cheeks with gentle hands and stroking her soft skin with his thumb-pads.

When her eyes filled with tears Byron was appalled at himself.

'What's wrong?' he asked. He could no longer deny his feelings for this woman. He was definitely falling in love with her.

'No, no, please don't cry,' he groaned, rubbing the tears away with his hands. 'I'll start crying if you keep crying.'

That startled her into stopping. '*You*, Byron?'

'Yes, me. I can be a real cry-baby. I cried for days when my parents divorced.'

'Did you cry when you broke up with your fiancée recently?'

Good Lord, why did she bring that up? 'Not for a second,' he said with a wry laugh. 'My only emotion at that time was relief. And some lingering anger over what a fool I'd been to be taken in by an obvious gold-digger for a second time in a row.'

She sighed. 'They both probably told you that they loved you.'

'All the time.'

'But their actions spoke louder than words.'

'Spot on.'

Her smile carried a strange sadness. 'I promise I won't tell you that I love you.'

Byron's gut squeezed tight for a telling moment, but he kept a nonchalant expression. 'Feel free. I won't mind. Like I said, I'm a romantic.'

She stared at him long and hard, then shrugged. 'Now that would be silly of me, don't you think? You have enough power over me without admitting such a thing.'

Byron's breath caught in his throat. Did she realise what she'd just said? It made his hopes soar and his heart do a tango.

'And what power do I have over you, my darling?' he crooned as he pulled her down on top of him.

Her sigh carried the most delicious sound of surrender. 'You make me do things which I know are unwise,' she said, and buried her face into the base of his throat.

'Like what?'

'Like this…'

Byron groaned when she opened her lips against his skin and began to suck.

CHAPTER TWENTY-ONE

MONDAY MORNING FOUND Cleo in a dilemma over what she was going to wear to work. She hadn't fully tackled her working wardrobe last Friday, concentrating on the outfit she was to wear on the Saturday night, plus some stylish casual clothes. Grace *had* talked her into buying one outrageously expensive pant suit suitable for any occasion, but it was white!

No. She wasn't going to wear white to work. But she really had to go out and buy some new work clothes. *Today.*

Very reluctantly, Cleo drew on her grey pant suit, teaming it with her one of her crisp white shirts. Only her shoes were new. Italian, and still black, but with a high heel. Despite the heels, however, they were wonderfully comfortable and cripplingly expensive. Cleo slipped her feet into them, noticing immediately the difference they made. She stood taller, with more style. Her walk became sexier. Once she made up her face and left her hair down, she didn't look half bad. Spraying herself with perfume, she entered the kitchen with a sauciness in her step, Doreen raising her eyebrows at her appearance.

'Is that suit new?' she asked.

'No,' Cleo returned brightly, and bent to stroke a waiting Mungo. 'But the woman wearing it is.'

She'd woken this morning still experiencing some anxiety over her relationship with Byron, but eventually deciding not to worry about something she had no control over.

Just enjoy yourself while it lasts, girl, was her new mantra.

'I have to admit I was wrong about that man,' Doreen said. 'He's been very good for you.'

'And I know another man who's been very good for *you*,' Cleo countered. 'And I don't mean Mungo here. Even if he is a dear.' She stroked his big ugly head some more.

When Doreen blushed, Cleo knew she wasn't the only one in this kitchen with her emotions in turmoil.

Cleo left for work in an optimistic frame of mind. Life, she decided as she strode down her street towards the railway station, was, indeed, wonderful. She didn't bury her head in the morning paper during the ride into town, as she usually did. Instead, she people watched, wondering if they felt as happy as she did that morning.

'Looking good, boss,' Leanne chirped when Cleo walked through Reception.

'You too, Leanne,' she returned warmly, after a moment's hesitation. She wasn't used to being complimented on her appearance. But it made her doubly determined to do some more clothes shopping at lunchtime. She now knew what shops to go to, thanks to Grace.

I really should ring and thank her personally, Cleo

thought as she sat down and opened her laptop. Before *I start checking emails.* And taking phone calls from harassed managers, all panicking because Scott was still away.

Without hesitating this time, she picked up her phone and brought up Grace's number, pressing call immediately.

'Hi there, Cleo,' Grace answered in that super-cool, composed manner of hers. Cleo couldn't imagine anything ever fazing Grace. She was the ultimate PA, and the nicest, kindest lady.

'I'm very well, thank you,' Cleo said. 'Which is why I'm ringing. To thank you for all your help, and your advice.'

'I take it you were a big hit on Saturday night?'

'I think I passed muster with his mother.' At least, she hoped so. She also hoped the woman hadn't noticed they'd left early. It suddenly occurred to her to ask Byron if he'd been in contact with his mother since the party. He hadn't said anything last night and she hadn't thought to ask. Her mind had been on other things.

'And what about with Byron? Did he like the way you looked?' Grace laughed. 'Silly question. He'd have been drooling.'

'He did seem pleased.' If ever there was an understatement that was it. 'Is he in yet?'

'No, actually, he isn't. But that's not surprising. Byron is not a Monday morning person. He'll be in shortly, I dare say. By the way, I was reading the financial section of the paper over breakfast and the iron ore prices have gone up. Coal, too. And gold, of course.'

Yipes! Cleo bit her bottom lip. *She* was the one who should have been doing that, instead of sitting there on the train with her head in the clouds. She hadn't even bought a paper this morning, which had been very slack of her. Scott had trusted her to keep her finger on the pulse and she'd been off in dreamland, having makeovers and inappropriate affairs. They did say you shouldn't mix business with pleasure—this was clearly why.

'Yes, I did notice that,' she lied. 'Byron might have missed the boat,' she added, covering her tracks well. 'Scott might not need a new partner after all. Oops, I shouldn't have said that. Don't tell Byron I said that. Please, Grace.'

'My lips are sealed. And, Cleo…'

'Yes?'

'I know it's none of my business, but did Byron ask you out again after Saturday night?'

'We had dinner together last night,' she admitted cagily.

'That's great. You've no idea how pleased I am that you and Byron have hit it off. He really needs to be with someone decent like you after those two fortune hunters he was involved with.'

'I still can't believe he's attracted to me.' Even *before* her makeover, if Byron was to be believed.

'I can.'

'Then *explain* it to me.'

'I just did. You're the genuine article, Cleo. Not a fake. And you were always extremely attractive, even in that ghastly black suit and those truly awful shoes. I hope you're wearing your new shoes today.'

'I certainly am. With what they cost, I plan to wear them every single day!'

'Good shoes are an investment. So is a good white pant suit. But I'll bet you're not wearing it today, are you?'

'No. I was too afraid to. It might get dirty.'

'That's what dry-cleaning is for, Cleo.'

'I know, Grace. I know. But even Rome wasn't built in a day.'

'You have thrown out that awful black suit and shoes, haven't you?'

Cleo grimaced. 'They're already in the charity shop bag.'

'Good. Now I must go. Byron is headed my way. Bye.'

Byron wasn't in a good mood. He hated that what he wanted remained just beyond his reach. Hated that the woman he was pursuing was being determinedly distant. Their final lovemaking session last night had reinforced his fear that her only priority where he was concerned was sex, sex, and more sex. As much as that had its exciting aspects, it was no longer satisfying his male ego. Why hadn't she fallen in love with him, damn it? Almost every other woman did.

'Morning, Grace,' he grumped as he strode past.

'Good morning, Byron,' came her perfectly polite reply, yet delivered with a faint smirk on her lips and a knowing glint in her eye.

He spun around and ground to a halt just beyond her desk, spearing her with narrowed eyes.

'Okay. Spit it out, Grace, so that I can get on with my day without worrying about what you know that I don't.'

Now her face was all blank innocence. 'I have no idea what you're talking about.'

His lips pressed together in frustration.

'I used to like women, but I'm beginning to think they were put on this earth to make us men miserable.'

'Are you referring to any one woman in particular? Or women in general?'

Byron laughed. 'You don't get to trap me that easily, Grace. You just do your job and mind your own damned business.'

His fury and his frustration bubbling over, he whirled and marched into his office. Five minutes later, he was calling Grace in.

'I apologise,' he said, shamed by his earlier rudeness.

'Apology accepted,' Grace replied without a shred of resentment in her voice.

'That's what I like about you, Grace. Nothing I do offends you.'

'That's because you're my boss. Now, if my husband spoke to me like that, I'd eat him alive. But don't push it. Even I have my limits. Now I suggest you ring Cleo before you explode.'

Byron's mouth dropped open 'How did you…?'

'Just ring her,' Grace said firmly, then left him to it.

Shrugging, Byron reached for his phone.

'But I *can't* go out to dinner with you again tonight,' Cleo told Byron.

She'd been perusing the financial pages of the morning paper when he rang, his invitation coming hot on the heels of his hello.

'Doreen goes to trivia down at the local on a Monday night,' she explained, 'and I'm certainly not going to ask her to give it up. I can't expect her to do all the work looking after Mungo. It's not right.'

Cleo held her breath when there was dead silence on the line.

'I see,' he said at last. 'Would you have any objections to me coming over and minding Mungo with you, then?'

Cleo had to stop herself from agreeing straight away but she couldn't help being secretly thrilled. Oh, dear... She was getting in deeper and deeper, wasn't she? As much as she'd vowed to enjoy their affair for what it was, she simply couldn't just go along with *everything* he wanted, could she? She'd resolved early on not to become a yes girl. And she meant to keep to that resolve. Give a man like Byron an inch and he would take a mile!

'That would be nice,' she said. 'But no sex, Byron,' she added firmly. Every time they made love, her feelings for him escalated. *She* was the one who hadn't been able to control herself last night. At times, she'd wanted to eat him alive, to drink him in and draw him into her very soul.

'It won't be me who breaks that rule, madam,' Byron said with a rueful laugh in his voice. 'Who was it who couldn't stop last night? Frankly, I don't think I could get it up today if I tried.'

'Oh,' she said, hating her dismay.

'Only kidding. I'm sitting here right now with a rod of iron, just waiting for you. We'll make out on the sofa and Mungo can close his eyes.'

'Cleo?' he said, when she said nothing. She couldn't. She was fully occupied, thinking about his rod of iron.

'Yes?' she squeaked.

'What time tonight do you want me there?'

'I… I can't think…'

'I like the sound of that,' he murmured in a far too seductive voice. 'Want to try some phone sex?'

She was tempted. Oh, how she was tempted. Which annoyed her.

'For pity's sake, Byron, have some decorum. I'm in charge here. I have work to do. And speaking of work, do you think you might tell me soon if you're still interested in investing in McAllister Mines? Scott is sure to ring me today for an update on that,' she lied, desperate to know if he'd seen the price rises in minerals or not.

A weary-sounding sigh wafted down the line. 'I haven't made up my mind on that, yet.'

'I see. Well, when can I expect a decision?'

'Soon,' he said, not very helpfully.

'How soon is soon?'

'Maybe in another couple of weeks. I need to do a little more research on the subject. And I would like to talk to Scott personally. When did you say he was getting back?'

'Er… I'm not quite sure.'

'Then ask him when he rings today.'

Cleo rolled her eyes. Trust her to get caught out in her lie.

'Okay,' she said. 'Now I really must go.'

'What time do you want me at your place tonight?' he asked before she could escape.

'What? Oh, yes. Tonight. How about seven-thirty?'

'Are you going to feed me, or do you want me to bring something?'

'I suppose I'll feed you. If you promise to be a good boy.'

'Oh, I'll be good,' he said smugly. 'Very, *very* good.'

CHAPTER TWENTY-TWO

AND THAT WAS how the working week continued, with Cleo doing her best to stop Byron from having his wicked way with her at some stage every day, but failing dismally.

When she begged off having dinner with him on Tuesday, he showed up in her office at lunchtime and swept her into Scott's inner sanctum, where he locked the door and proceeded to make her act with an appalling lack of respect for her boss's desk.

On Wednesday evening, he helped her mind Mungo again whilst Doreen went out with Harvey to the movies. They started to watch a movie themselves on the TV but ended up—as they had on the Monday evening—making out on the sofa. Mungo by then tolerated Byron without barking, but he still wasn't keen on him. The dog adored Harvey, however, which was just as well, since Harvey made any and every excuse to visit.

Thursday, Byron took Cleo food shopping at the local supermarket whilst Doreen put on a baked lamb dinner, supervised by a salivating Mungo, and the ever-attentive Harvey who'd brought two bottles of superb red wine for them all to drink. By eight-thirty, the four of them were seated at the small square dining table, with their wine glasses in hand and smiles all around.

Cleo's smile, however, was false, her pragmatic and positive mood earlier in the week now spoiled by the nagging worry about where this would all end. Not for Harvey and Doreen. She could see they were headed for the altar. She and Byron were a different story altogether. Yes, he was enjoying playing at being a regular couple. But it was just playing. She was sure of it. Once he grew bored with the game, he would move on. He also wouldn't end up becoming a partner of McAllister Mines, despite the resurgence in mineral prices. When she'd told him Scott wouldn't be back for another two weeks—she'd had to fabricate a return date—he hadn't seemed overly concerned. Neither had he wanted to discuss the business with her. You didn't have to be a genius to work out why. His priority wasn't business with her. It was pleasure.

Cleo could not deny that it was very pleasurable, being with him. He was a witty and charming companion as well as a fantastic lover. He wasn't nearly as arrogant as she'd first imagined, but he could still be quite domineering, and insistent on getting his own way. Given how she felt about him, Cleo worried that she would give in too often, and, after finally blossoming with her new independence and self-confidence, she couldn't bear to go back to the way she used to be. She managed to enforce her own wishes occasionally, but underneath she knew he was way out of her league. Even with her revamped appearance, Cleo knew nothing could make her believe he would ever think of her as a suitable partner for life.

But did she really want that, anyway? Hadn't she always believed she would never remarry? Would never give any man power over her life again?

She certainly had until Byron came along.

Now, she spent every night lying in bed, dreaming of him declaring his love and asking her to marry him. And she despised herself for it.

A foolish pipe dream, she accepted, as she looked across the table at Byron, dressed tonight in dark trousers and a blue sweater, the same colour as his eyes. How handsome he was. Handsome and confident and, oh, so unattainable. He liked her, yes. A lot. And he liked making love to her. A lot. But he wasn't in love with her.

A man in love would surely tell her so. Often. His silence on the subject was very telling. And very sobering.

Smothering a sigh, Cleo put down her wine glass and picked up her knife and fork.

Byron wondered what that sigh meant. What had she been thinking about when her gaze had travelled over him, oh, so thoughtfully, and slightly sadly?

He didn't know. She wasn't like the women he was used to, regaling him with stories about her life when they were alone. Or asking him endless questions about previous girlfriends. He suspected she still didn't consider herself a proper girlfriend. She was just his lover. No, *he* was just *her* lover. Their relationship wasn't real to her. It was just a fling. A sexual fantasy maybe. To be kept separate from her *real* life.

For some reason, Byron didn't like the role of fantasy lover. So he'd tried to change her attitude this past week, tried to make her confide in him like a friend, asking her questions whilst they lay in bed together, naked and intimate. But it wasn't working. She remained at a distance from him. Emotionally, not physically. Physically, she was his. But what good was that in the long run? He wanted her body and soul. He wanted her love. The only way he would know for sure that he would be able to trust his feelings for her would be if she returned them in equal measure.

The time had come to show his hand more forcefully.

'That was a fantastic meal, Doreen,' he said after they'd polished off dessert, a mouth-watering caramel pie with whipped cream. 'Would you consider me rude if I skipped coffee and took Cleo out for a drive? I have some important business I want to discuss with her.'

Cleo bristled at the way he talked as though she weren't in the room, not to mention his typically male suggestion that she just leave Doreen to clean up everything. They had a rule in their house. The person who cooked didn't do the clearing up.

'I wouldn't dream of leaving Doreen to do all the clearing away,' she told him sharply. 'Perhaps we can discuss it while we clear up together?'

'Don't be silly,' Doreen jumped in immediately. 'Harvey and I can load the dishwasher. It's no big deal. You two go. I insist.'

'She insists,' Harvey repeated when Cleo just sat there, a mutinous expression on her face.

'Cleo?' Byron prodded, and stood up.

Cleo rose to her feet with great reluctance, not wanting to make a scene.

'Has it occurred to you that maybe Harvey and Doreen wanted to be alone too?' Byron said quietly on their way to his car.

'Not really,' she bit out. 'I doubt it occurred to you, either. Until just now. So what's this important business you want to discuss with me?' she went on, pretty sure she knew what it was. He didn't want to invest in McAllister Mines any longer.

Or in her.

'For pity's sake, Cleo, just stop it,' he snapped, and turned her to face him.

'Stop what?'

He dragged her against him and kissed her; kissed her until her head was reeling and her body was on fire for him. He wrenched his mouth away, leaving her bereft, and confused. His heated glare was one of anger, rather than passion.

'Just get in the car,' he commanded, letting her go in order to reef open the passenger door.

She got in, dazed into blind obedience.

'Put the damned seat belt on,' he ordered once he was behind the wheel.

She put the seat belt on.

'Now don't say a single word until I get myself under control again. I'll let you know when that happens. Can you manage to do that without arguing with me?'

She nodded.

'Good.'

It took Cleo a while to get herself under control again as well, to calm her throbbing body, and her whirling mind. She stared blankly out at the inner-city lights as Byron drove the now familiar route to his building, the one that housed his office and his penthouse. By the time he zoomed down into the underground car park, she felt passably composed. But still totally confused, and on the cusp of anger. What did he want to discuss with her? She doubted it could be about business. That could have waited till the morning. It had to be personal. Were those kisses goodbye kisses? Was he bringing her here for goodbye sex before dumping her? If that was it, then he could just go jump off that terrace of his. In fact, she might push him off herself. He had been insufferably rude, and she was determined not to let him get away with it. Cleo Shelton was no pushover, not any more anyway.

'Can I talk now?' she said when he turned off the engine. It amazed her how controlled her voice was. Not a tremble in sight. All the trembling was deep inside.

'If you must,' he threw back at her.

'Just be honest with me,' she said firmly. 'If you don't want to see me any more, then just say so.'

His stare seemed shocked. 'Not want to see you any more? Are you insane? The truth is just the opposite. I want to see you every day of my life. As my wife. I want to marry you, Cleo. That's what I wanted to talk to you about. I've been telling myself to be patient, but when I spoke to Dad about my feelings for you today he said I was an idiot to wait. That I should speak up and tell you how I feel about you. I've fallen madly in love with you, Cleo. Can't you see that?'

Cleo didn't know what to say, her reaction to Byron's declaration of love—plus his astonishing proposal—not even close to the reaction she had in her secret fantasies over such a thing happening. Rather than being over the moon, she was immediately beset with huge doubts and fears. His use of the words *madly in love* conjured up a love that wasn't stable; that couldn't last. He'd probably been *madly in love* with his two previous fiancées. And where had they ended up? On the scrapheap. Aside from that, Cleo knew deep down that she wasn't the sort of woman he'd always planned to marry. Yes, she looked presentable enough now that she'd smartened herself up and bought some flattering clothes. But that was all just surface stuff. Cleo felt she didn't have what it took to be Byron's wife. Neither was she at all sure that she even *wanted* to be Byron's wife. She didn't want to give up her job and become some kind of society hostess. Neither did she want to sit at home with the children whilst he travelled around the world and negotiated business deals worth billions.

Byron was a powerful man who would expect his wife to be subservient to him and his wishes. She couldn't do that. Not again. She would *never* do that. Which meant any marriage between them would be doomed from the start. Better to have her heart broken now than later.

When she slowly shook her head from side to side, he reached over to cup her face and turn it towards him, his eyes searching hers. 'Don't you love me, Cleo?' he asked. 'Is that it?'

Her face twisted, as did her heart. 'Of course I love you,' she choked, saddened beyond belief at her perverse response to his words.

The joy—the relief—that exploded through Byron's chest was off the Richter scale.

'What's the problem, then?' he asked as he let her face go and slumped back into the driver's seat.

'The problem is *I* don't want to marry *you*, Byron.'

Panic was just a heartbeat away. If she didn't marry him then he would never get married. Cleo was all he wanted now. No one else would do.

'Why not?' he asked, trying to keep his cool when he was anything but.

'You'll try to change me, Byron. I know you will.'

'Why would I want to change you when it is you that I fell in love with?'

'Marriage changes men,' she stated, her eyes clouding with unhappy memories.

Byron knew then for sure that her first marriage had not been idyllic.

'You'll want me to give up my job for starters,' she went on.

'I promise I won't,' he bit out.

'Promises are made to be broken. And so are vows. A man like you, Byron, will find it hard to stay faithful, especially once the gloss wears off and you grow bored with me.'

'I will never grow bored with you.'

'You will…'

'So you're saying no to my proposal?'

'I have to.'

Byron's hands lifted to scrape through his hair in total frustration. He felt like tearing it out by the roots, but he didn't, his hands dropping back to clasp the wheel instead. He had no intention of giving up. Giving up was not in his nature.

'Right,' he said, adopting his best negotiating voice as he dropped his hands into his lap and turned to face her, his expression neutral. 'I see now that I've made a mistake. I've rushed you.' His father's advice had been misguided. He should have waited before proposing. After all, they'd only known each other a little over a week.

Had it really only been that long? It had felt much longer. Falling madly in love like this made every second of every day seem like an eternity, filled with longing and need, plus the kind of wonderful dreams that demanded to be made real, and permanent. Love wasn't patient, Byron realised. It made mistakes.

'How about moving in with me for a while?' he suggested instead. 'What do you say to that?'

Cleo had to admire his persistence. As well as her own level-headedness at being able to turn it down. Maybe that was what came with having been married before, in knowing the pitfalls of just saying yes to a man all the time. She knew it was probably a case of *once bitten twice shy*, but she couldn't help it. She couldn't go through what she'd experienced with Martin ever again. If she was to eventually agree to marry Byron—and it was still a big if—then he had to know up front that she would not change for him. Not in the things that mattered to her.

'I'm sorry, Byron,' she said, moved by his immediately crestfallen face. But not moved enough to change her mind. 'I would prefer that we just continue as we are until I know you better.'

His lips pouted with that boyish anger she'd glimpsed once or twice. 'What more is there for you to know?' he snapped. 'You've already done a full security check on me. I'm an open book. I'm also a good catch, if you haven't noticed. I can give you anything money can buy. I do realise that a penthouse is not the right kind of residence for a couple who want children, but...' He broke off and gave a savage glance. 'Is that it? You don't want children?'

'No, that's not it, Byron. I would love to have a child. I already told you that. I just won't have a baby outside of marriage. I know women have babies on their own all the time, but I've always believed children are happier with two happily married parents to bring them up.'

'I fully agree with you on that score,' he said. 'I was devastated when my parents divorced, though I did have the good fortune to have them seemingly happy together for the first sixteen years of my life. Lara wasn't so fortunate. And it shows. She's somewhat of a rebel. She's terribly spoiled, of course. Mum spoils her. Guilt, you see.'

'Over the divorce?'

'In a way.' He shot Cleo a thoughtful look. 'This is strictly in confidence. But you might as well know, as the future Mrs Byron Maddox. Best to start as I mean to go on. Without secrets.'

Cleo rolled her eyes but decided to let that pass.

'Lara's not Dad's biological daughter,' Byron went on.

'Mum had an affair with her tennis coach. Very cliché, I know, but it's the truth.'

'Goodness!' Cleo exclaimed. 'Does Lara know?'

'No. The real father doesn't know, either. Dad said he'd accept her as his own in exchange for a no contest divorce.'

'How come you know? Did your mum tell you?'

'No. Dad came clean after I started playing up at university. I was angry with him, you see. Anyway, we sorted things out and we're now closer than ever, despite our differences,' he added laughingly. 'I don't like the way he does business sometimes, and he thinks I'm far too careful with my money. Which reminds me. I don't want to invest in McAllister Mines, despite the rise in mineral prices. It's just not me. I'm going into the movie business instead.'

'And you call that being careful with your money,' she said, smiling.

'I know what you mean. But Blake Randall is looking for a silent partner in his production company and I told him today that I'm in. I'm sorry about that, but I suspect your boss will survive now that things have improved on the mining front. *Now*…what say we go upstairs and get to know each other better in the biblical sense?'

Cleo's stomach tightened, as did her heart. Oh, how she wished that she could be as pragmatic with this proposal as she'd been with his earlier one. But it was impossible. This was one area where she simply couldn't say no to the man she loved.

'Coming?' he said.

Always, she thought as her nipples hardened and her lower half went to mush.

CHAPTER TWENTY-THREE

CLEO FELT THE evidence when she went to the bathroom in the middle of the night. They'd made love on and off for hours, Byron seemingly insatiable. And highly imaginative, choosing positions that were satisfying but hardly romantic. Only once had they made love face to face. That had been the first time. After that, he'd turned her over and played with her for ages before pulling her up on all fours. Then later, when she'd been almost comatose with satisfaction and fatigue, he'd slipped into her in the spoon position. He'd fallen asleep soon after coming that time, but she hadn't, kept awake by an urgent need to go to the toilet.

Even the act of walking into the bathroom had given rise to suspicion. She didn't normally feel this *icky* after sex with Byron. He always used condoms, after all. She hoped it was only her natural lubrication sticking to her thighs, but she feared not. When she sat down, more liquid poured out of her.

Oh, God…

Her heart plummeted as the realisation hit that she and Byron had had unprotected sex. It must have been a mistake. But Byron wasn't the sort of man to make that kind of mistake. Had he really meant to do it? Was that why he'd chosen those positions, so she wouldn't notice his lack of protection? Had he really been trying to get her pregnant, to trap her into marriage with him?

Cleo felt sick. Not because she was afraid she might have fallen pregnant. Her period was due in a couple of days and she was never late so a pregnancy wasn't on the cards. No, her distress came from the fact that he would do such a thing. That he thought he could control her. Or force her to change her mind. With a baby, no less!

Fury rose in her chest so that she wanted to scream out loud. She almost did, opening her mouth in a silent scream as she clenched her fists and screwed up her face in an expression of utter despair. Because for Byron to do such a thing showed total ruthlessness and selfishness. Which meant he would never be the man for her. *Never!* What'd he'd done was very wrong, evoking all her old tapes from her marriage to Martin. She could not go there a second time. Never ever, no matter how much she loved Byron. She would rather spend the rest of her life alone. Neither could she let him get away with such behaviour. It just wasn't right.

But first, she had a shower, practically scrubbing herself red raw in self-righteous fury before donning one of the white towelling robes that Byron kept in the bathroom and marching out to do battle with her new enemy.

Byron woke to Cleo shaking his shoulder rather roughly.

'Wake up, you bastard,' she threw at him, her angry

words propelling him into instant wakefulness. And clarity.

Man, but she was mad at him. Spitting mad.

Byron groaned. He hadn't meant to have unsafe sex with her. He'd been half asleep with his body spooned around hers when she'd wriggled back against him and he'd just reacted instinctively. He'd been inside her before he could think straight. When his brain had kicked into gear he'd convinced himself that it wouldn't matter if she did fall pregnant; he loved her, wanted to marry her, and wanted to have a child with her. What was the problem?

'Did you honestly think you were going to get away with it?' she snapped. 'Did you think I wouldn't notice great gallops of sperm running down my legs?'

Byron flinched at her rather crude description.

'I'm sorry,' was all he could think of to say. 'It was only that last time. I didn't mean to. Honestly. I was half asleep…'

'I don't believe you,' she snapped. 'You did mean it. I know you, Byron. You don't like taking no for an answer. I turned down your proposal so you tried for a shotgun wedding instead.'

'That wasn't my intention,' Byron declared heatedly. 'But if you have fallen pregnant, then is that so bad? I love you, Cleo, and I want to marry you. And have babies with you. Look, once I realised what I was doing, it was too late to pull out. And I thought…well, I thought…'

'If you'd *thought*,' she ground out, her cheeks dotted with angry red spots, 'if you knew me at *all*, you'd know that what you did tonight would make me run so fast in the opposite direction, even your father's fancy jet couldn't catch up. But, of course, you don't know me, do you? Not really. You might have, if you'd been patient, but no, you couldn't wait for that to happen. Not Byron Maddox, who has to have what he wants when he wants it. So you tried to force me to marry you, using a poor, innocent little baby to do that. Never mind how I might have felt about falling pregnant.'

'Cleo, I—'

'Not one word, Byron! I can't stand the words that come out of your treacherous mouth. You say you love me but you have no concept of true love. All you know is what *you* want. Never mind anyone else's feelings. Other people are just here to fulfil your needs, especially women. I feel sorry for those two girls you were once engaged to. They probably thought you cared about them. But you didn't. They just fed your ego for a while. Well, I have no intention of taking over from them, Byron. I'm not in the business of feeding your ego. Now, I'm going to get dressed and go home. No, please don't get up. I'll call a taxi. Frankly, I don't want to spend one single second in your, oh, so charming company.'

'For pity's sake, Cleo,' he started as she scooped up her clothes and carried them in the direction of the bathroom.

She whirled on him. 'I have no pity for you. You are dead in my eyes. Dead and gone.'

'You don't mean that,' he said, horrified by the coldness in her face.

'Trust me. I do.'

'But you love me.'

She laughed. 'More fool me. But I'll get over you in time. Trust me on that, too.'

His eyes narrowed. She couldn't mean that. She couldn't!

'You're just angry at the moment. I'll call you tomorrow.'

'Don't. I'm warning you. You'll be wasting your time.'

'Then it's my time to waste,' he ground out, angry now himself. Okay, what he'd done had been stupid, but there was no harm done. Byron suspected that her anger wasn't entirely directed at him. The bottom line, however, was that she loved him. He could feel that love every time they were in bed together. So he wasn't going to give up on her. He couldn't. She was the woman he wanted and he wasn't about to roll over like some whipped dog and just let her go.

'I'll be in touch,' he told her again even as she banged the bathroom door shut.

When she came out fully dressed he didn't say a word. He watched in silence as she called a taxi, his heart heavy with regret as he watched her leave. If only he could go back in time, he would have stopped and reached for a damned condom. Now, he'd made his mission of winning Cleo extremely difficult.

But not impossible, he decided with a burst of renewed optimism. Nothing was impossible. Not if you really truly loved a person. And they really truly loved you in return. She would forgive him in time. Surely.

Because the alternative didn't bear thinking about.

CHAPTER TWENTY-FOUR

CLEO HAD NOT long sat down at her desk the following Wednesday morning when Harvey walked in, carrying a vase of two dozen long-stemmed red roses.

'The delivery guy was hovering in Reception when I came through,' he explained. 'From Byron, I presume?'

'Yes,' Cleo said frostily. 'He sends me the same thing at the same time every day. This is the sixth day in a row.' He'd had them delivered to her home over the weekend. 'I'll have Leanne send them over to the women's hospital. That's what I did with the other ones.' The roses at the weekend had been put straight into the bin, much to Doreen's horror. But Cleo simply couldn't bear to look at them.

Harvey put the vase down on her desk, then picked up the attached envelope but didn't open it. 'What does the card say?'

'Always the same thing,' she bit out. '"I'm sorry. I love you. Please forgive me."'

'So why don't you?'

Cleo stiffened. 'I just can't.'

'No, you just *won't*.'

'If you say so.'

'I do say so. Don't let your pride get in the way of forgiving the man, Cleo.'

'It's not a question of pride, Harvey. Now, is there
anything I can do for you?'

'Nope. Just came to tell you that Doreen's worried
about you. She says you're not eating properly. Or sleeping.'

Not entirely true. She did sleep, but only with the help
of some sleeping tablets she'd been prescribed after Martin's death. They did the trick, but she still woke, feeling
exhausted and emotionally drained. It annoyed her that
Doreen had spoken to Harvey and not her.

'Then why doesn't she say so herself?'

Harvey shrugged. 'Doreen's not good at confronta-
tion. Look, she told me all about the way her husband
treated her and it doesn't take much brains to work out
her son was just the same.'

'He was,' Cleo agreed, her chest tightening.

'Byron shouldn't have to suffer for what another man
did.'

'He's not. He's suffering for what *he* did.'

'Right, well, I don't know anything about that. But I
guess it's your life. You have the right to stuff it up, if
that's what you want. I told Doreen I'd try to talk some
sense into you and I have. Mission accomplished. So,
when's the boss getting back?'

'He should be in any time now. His plane landed at
six-thirty this morning. He sent a text saying he'd go
home first and freshen up, then come straight in.'

'What are you going to tell him about Maddox?'

'The truth,' Cleo said tautly. 'That Byron isn't interested in a partnership with him.'

Harvey laughed. 'Good luck with that. Scott might be a bit thick at times but he's no fool. He only has to take one look at you to know that something's been going on with you and Maddox. And I'm not talking about your new wardrobe and hairstyle. It's all there in your eyes every time the man is mentioned.'

'Oh,' she said, those betraying eyes of hers immediately smarting with tears. She rapidly blinked them away, lifting her chin in defiance of her emotional response, tapping into the hurt that still raged inside her. 'Thank you for telling me that,' she said. 'I'll be on my guard in future.'

Harvey rolled his eyes. 'I'm just glad it brought me Doreen. She's one sweet, loving woman.'

'Yes, she is. And if you ever hurt her you'll have me to answer to.'

Harvey nodded. 'I can believe that. But you don't have to worry. I would never hurt Doreen. I love her even more than I love my Harley-Davidson. And that's saying something. In fact, I…'

The arrival of Scott, accompanied by his wife, Sarah, put paid to that conversation. Harvey made the right noises before hurrying off, leaving Cleo to face the couple who were staring at her, totally gobsmacked by her appearance.

Cleo was wearing her stunning new white pant suit. Her hair was up, but in a less severe style than the old days. And she was wearing lots of make-up, plus the reddest lipstick. All in defiance of her inner unhappiness, of course.

Sarah was the first to put two and two together and get five, her eyes going from Cleo to the red roses then back to Cleo again.

'Someone has got herself an admirer,' she exclaimed. 'And a new look to go with it. Am I right, or am I right?'

'Sort of,' Cleo replied, not ready to explain all to her boss's wife. She liked Sarah, who was both beautiful and bright, but just a little bit overwhelming at times. In the past, Cleo had felt inferior to Sarah, with her innate style and bubbly personality. She was not in the mood today to confess all. Harvey's visit had left her on edge and questioning whether she was doing the right thing in not forgiving Byron. It was a struggle enough to stop herself from bursting into tears.

'Oh, do tell.'

'I…er…don't think…'

'For pity's sake, Sarah,' Scott said, indulgently. 'You came in here to give Cleo that pretty scarf you bought her, not put her through the third degree. Though I have to admit, Cleo, that you do look amazing. He must be an incredible man to make you go to so much trouble.'

That did it. Because Byron *was* incredible, really. If he hadn't done what he'd done, she'd probably be engaged to him right now and looking forward to a wonderful life together. Instead, she was sitting here with a future as lonely as it was bitter and sad.

She didn't start sobbing, but silent tears ran down her face, Cleo glimpsing the appalled expressions of Scott and Sarah before she buried her face in her hands.

It was Sarah who put her arms around Cleo's shoulders, holding her gently but firmly.

'Scott, go and get that box of tissues you keep on your desk,' Cleo heard her tell her husband.

Sarah mopped her up, then sent Scott off again to get them all coffee. But he was back within seconds, saying he'd given Leanne the job.

Cleo groaned. She didn't want everyone at work to know she was a mess. Though she supposed Leanne already knew, what with the flowers and all.

'I think what Cleo really needs,' Sarah said decisively, 'is to get out of this office for a while. Come on, sweetie, we'll go for a walk and find a nice place where we can sit and have a girl-to-girl chat.'

'But I was hoping to talk to Cleo about business!' Scott protested. 'I need an update on the Byron Maddox situation, asap.'

Just the mention of his name brought another groan from Cleo.

Sarah didn't need to be a genius to twig. Scott, however, being a typical man, still looked mystified.

'You won't be doing business with Byron bloody Maddox,' Sarah snapped. 'Not if I can help it.'

'But that's just it,' Scott said, his expression still perplexed. 'I don't need to now. McAllister Mines can survive without him.'

'Good,' Sarah bit out. 'Then just ring the man yourself and tell him that. Now, Cleo and I are going out for coffee. And we won't be back for a good while.'

'But Leanne's just gone to get us all coffee,' he pointed out frustratedly.

Sarah merely rolled her eyes and led Cleo out.

Cleo knew that Sarah could be quite formidable when

she wanted to be, recalling how she'd left Scott not that long ago, refusing to return to him until Cleo had stepped in herself and begged Sarah to give him a second chance. Which she had. But on her own terms. Cleo admired her enormously. It would be good to talk to someone who would understand her own stance.

But she didn't understand. Not even remotely.

'So he asked you to marry him and you said not yet. And then he proceeded to have sex with you without a condom and, once you realised, you had a big hissy fit and then you broke up with him, even though you weren't likely to get pregnant. Did I get that right?'

'Well, yes,' Cleo said, glancing around the rather crowded café, hoping that none of the other customers were listening in on their conversation.

'What he did wasn't that bad, Cleo. It doesn't rate compared with what Scott did to me. Byron didn't believe the worst about you. Or have vengeful sex. He just had unintentionally unsafe sex. And only the once. When he was half asleep, might I add. Now, if what you tell me is true, then he's really in love with you. I mean, he fancied you even when you looked nothing short of dreary. Sorry to say that but you did. Now, I can't say I thought all that much of Byron Maddox when I met him last year, but, if I'm brutally honest, I judged him by the truly ghastly girlfriend he was with. Stunning to look at but totally up herself. It was a case of dislike transference.'

'What?'

Sarah laughed. 'That's lawyer talk. It just comes out of my mouth sometimes. Now back to the point. You have to give the man a second chance, Cleo. Remember what you told me that night you came to see me when Scott and I were separated? You said marriage is hard. And it is. But very worthwhile, if your husband really truly loves you. And I think Byron really truly loves you. Not like your first husband,' she added, which brought Cleo up with a jolt.

'What makes you say that? Martin loved me.'

'Did he?'

'Yes, he did,' Cleo said, a great lump forming in her throat. 'In his own way...'

'And what way was that, Cleo?' she asked gently.

Cleo sighed, then told her everything, crying occasionally as she put all the horrors she'd endured during the early years of her marriage into words.

'What a bastard,' Sarah murmured.

'He didn't know any better,' Cleo said as she wiped her eyes. 'He was copying the way his father behaved.'

'That's no excuse, Cleo. You must know that.'

She nodded. 'I do. I was actually going to leave him, but then he got cancer and I just couldn't. He changed after that.'

'You mean he lost control over you.'

'Yes. Yes, that's exactly what happened.'

'But it left you afraid of men, and what they can do, if you give them power over you.'

'Yes,' she agreed with a long sigh.

'You have to tell Byron what you just told me. You have to make him understand how important it is to you that he never does anything like that again. That's another thing you told me that night—to be honest and upfront with your loved ones. Tell them what you want out of life and what you don't want. You do *want* children, don't you?'

'Yes. But having a baby has to be a mutual decision. I don't want to feel forced into anything.'

'Then tell Byron that. I'm sure he's ready to listen by now.'

'I… I don't know…'

Sarah crossed her arms and gave Cleo an uncompromising glare across the table. 'I'm not letting you out of that seat until you've rung the man and arranged to meet him.'

Cleo's lips pursed in automatic defiance. 'You can be seriously bossy, do you know that?'

'You made me promise the same thing with Scott, remember?'

'That was different,' Cleo argued.

'I don't see how.'

'You were already married.'

'It's being in love that matters. You do love Byron, don't you?'

'Yes…'

'Then get on your damned phone and ring the man.'

Cleo didn't move a muscle.

'I'm waiting,' Sarah said, her blue eyes as hard as flint.

Suddenly, Cleo thought of what Harvey had said that morning. *Don't let pride get in the way of your happiness.* Or something like that.

'All right,' she said, but when she rang, his number went to voicemail.

Dismayed, Cleo pressed Grace's number.

'Cleo,' Grace answered, sounding both surprised and delighted.

'I'm trying to contact Byron, Grace. Is he in?'

'No. He said he had to go out but didn't say where.'

'I see…'

'Have you tried ringing him?'

'His phone goes to voicemail.'

'I'm not surprised. He hasn't wanted to talk to anyone. He's very down, Cleo. Very…depressed.'

Cleo couldn't imagine Byron being down. Angry, yes. But not depressed.

'I'll let him know you called as soon as he gets back,' she offered.

'I'd appreciate that. And thanks for the roses.'

'What roses?'

Cleo had assumed that Byron would have had Grace organise the flowers. It distressed her that she'd been wrong, that she was so ready to believe the worst of Byron.

Just then Sarah's phone pinged, announcing a text message.

'I've found him!' Sarah exclaimed before Cleo could explain to Grace about the roses. 'He's with Scott, talking business. But Scott says he's just waiting until you get back.'

'It's all right. I heard that,' Grace piped up. 'Now for pity's sake, make up with him, Cleo. I can't stand another moment of the man. Honestly.'

Cleo smiled at the memory of how she'd felt exactly the same way when Scott had been fighting with

Sarah. He'd been the biggest misery. And impossible to work with.

'All right,' she said, and was immediately swamped by a wave of sheer joy.

'Let's get going,' she directed at Sarah. 'Bye, Grace.'

CHAPTER TWENTY-FIVE

BYRON STARTED DOOR-WATCHING after Scott contacted Sarah. The anticipation of seeing Cleo worried the life out of him, because he had no idea what kind of reception he'd receive. He'd had no response from his flowers. Not that he'd expected any really. She'd been too mad at him to fall for that ploy. But he'd had to do something, had to let her know how sorry he was. He'd resisted the frantic urge to bombard her with phone calls and text messages, giving her time for her anger to subside, hoping that the sight of the red roses might soften her stance.

By this morning, however, he could not stand to sit by and do nothing any longer. So he'd looked up the address of McAllister Mines' head office and walked up here, expecting to see Cleo, only to find that her boss had returned from his second honeymoon, and Cleo was out having coffee with his wife. Today's vase of red roses was still on her desk, however. Which gave him some hope.

'Are they coming back soon?' he asked Scott in an effort to soothe his escalating anxiety.

'They're on their way,' he replied before giving Byron

a searching look. 'So am I allowed to ask what you did that caused all this ruckus?'

'No.'

'That bad, eh? Well, it couldn't be as bad as what I did not that long ago, and Sarah and I are still together. If you truly love each other, things will work out in the end.'

Privately, Byron thought that was a very naive statement, coming from a grown man.

'I hope you're right about that,' he said.

'I know Cleo. She's got a lot of love in her. Do you know about her first marriage?'

Byron stiffened. 'I know a bit.'

'Sarah thinks her husband might not have treated her well.'

'I'm beginning to think the same thing.'

'They're back,' Scott whispered and stood up.

Byron did likewise, tensing at the sharp tap on the door.

'Come in, girls,' Scott called out.

Sarah came in first, looking delicious in bone trousers and an ice-blue mohair jumper. But Cleo trumped her in a stylish white pant suit, which complemented Cleo's dark colouring and brought life to her olive complexion. Around her neck hung a long turquoise chiffon scarf, which was bright but elegant. She looked surprisingly happy at the sight of him, only the red rims of her eyes betraying her recent distress.

'Hello, Byron,' Sarah said with a slight edge in her voice. 'I hear you've been a bad boy.'

Cleo winced whilst Byron held his breath.

'I think, my darling wife,' Scott said as he came

around and took Sarah's elbow, 'that Byron would like a private word with Cleo. So how about we both leave them alone for a while? We'll just be downstairs, Cleo. *Having coffee,*' he added with sarcasm. And before Sarah could protest, Scott ushered her out, shutting the door behind them.

'Tactful man, your boss,' Byron said as they stood there, staring at each other.

Cleo just stood there and drank Byron in. How handsome he was in that gorgeous dark blue suit. But then, he'd look gorgeous in anything. It surprised her, however, that his handsome face bore evidence of sleepless nights and real emotional distress. There were dark rings under his beautiful blue eyes and, if she wasn't mistaken, he'd lost weight, his cheeks just a little hollow underneath his cheekbones.

It saddened her that she'd made him suffer. She wasn't cruel. She was, however, a survivor. And as a survivor she had to make him understand why she'd been so hurt by what he'd done. He might not have planned it, but there had to have been a point when he could have stopped. Yet he hadn't. He'd gone right ahead, careless of the possible consequences and how she might feel about having a baby with him. Forgiving him was all very well, but it was only a starting point. If they had any chance of making it together as a couple, he had to know what she expected of him as her life partner: that he would never try to dominate her, control her, or manipulate her. She wanted to be an equal partner and refused to settle for anything less. But to be fair to him, he also had to know everything about her. Every single thing.

'I'm so sorry, Cleo,' he said before she could formulate where to begin.

She hoped her smile was a comfort to him. 'I know,' she said. 'And I forgive you.'

Hope lit his eyes. 'You do?'

'Yes. But that doesn't mean you weren't wrong. You were. *Very* wrong.'

'I know,' he said sincerely. 'If only I could go back in time…'

'That's the trouble with time. You can't go back. But I'm sorry too. I probably overreacted and I want to explain why.'

'I don't think you overreacted,' he muttered. 'I—'

'Oh, for pity's sake,' she interrupted. 'Will you just sit down and listen to me?'

Startled, he sat down in a nearby chair. Cleo moved around to sit in Scott's chair.

'Now,' she said, 'I'm going to tell you the story of a young girl who lost her parents in a car accident when she was just a teenager and went to live with her elderly grandparents who both died before she was nineteen, leaving her with no one to guide her, or to stop her from making the biggest mistake in her life.'

Cleo swallowed, then went on, not looking at Byron, keeping her eyes turned away and her voice as calm as she could make it. But it was hard to tell him everything, to leave nothing out. Not a single thing. She knew none of it was really her fault—circumstances had made her the perfect victim—but she still felt humiliated by what she had put up with during her marriage. By the time she got to the part where Martin died, silent tears were running down her cheeks. When Byron went to stand up she stopped him.

'Please don't,' she choked out. 'I haven't finished yet.'

He sank back down in his chair, his eyes kind and compassionate.

'After Martin died I vowed that I would never give a man that much control over my life ever again, that I would be truly independent. Which meant giving up my dream of having children, of being truly loved. Aside from my total lack of fashion sense, this was the main reason why I didn't really care how I looked. As long as I was neat and clean, I thought that was enough. But then you came along, and…and…'

Cleo broke off, unable to continue, her head shaking from side to side as she reached forward and grabbed a handful of tissues.

Byron's heart sank as he watched her weep. He ached to go to her. To hug her. Comfort her. But he sensed that was not the right course of action to achieve his goal. She needed a few moments to gather herself first.

Meanwhile, all Byron could do was work out what he *should* do. He had listened to Cleo's story with a mixture of sadness and admiration. How hard must it have been for her with no one to go to during the first years of her marriage; no one to tell her that the bastard she was married to was nothing more than a bully and a coward. Byron thought he'd got what he deserved. But Cleo didn't think so, or she wouldn't have stayed and cared for him. She was better than him, it was clear. Way more compassionate and forgiving. But she was also damaged.

Byron had once thought he didn't want to marry a woman who carried a lot of emotional baggage. Not now, however. Life without Cleo as his wife simply wasn't worth considering. If he couldn't have her then he didn't want anyone else. Besides, if he were brutally honest, he was damaged too. His parents' divorce had damaged him. His mother being unfaithful had damaged him. So had the realisation that his father was human and not some godlike figure on a pedestal.

Life damaged everyone in some way, Byron accepted. It was how you handled that damage that was the important thing.

'Can I speak now?' he said at last, his voice as calm as he could make it.

Cleo wiped her nose with a sigh. 'I suppose so.'

'I understand why you reacted the way you did to my not using a condom. I don't think it was an overreaction at all. It was very wrong of me to do that. I just want you to know that it definitely wasn't planned. It was an impulse, something that happened in the heat of the moment. Of course, there was a point when I knew I was risking you getting pregnant, but I selfishly thought how much I wanted to have a child with you. But I can see now how much you would have hated feeling that I'd deliberately tricked you, just to get what I wanted. I can see that I only thought of myself, and not about what *you* wanted, how *you* felt. I love you, my darling Cleo, and I desperately want to marry you. Please say yes. And please don't say that you don't love me, because I know you do.'

Her head shot up, her dark eyes widening. 'How do you know I meant it?'

'You said you forgave me.'

When Cleo felt her heart begin to melt she gritted her teeth, steadfastly refusing to surrender herself to his wishes that easily.

'Maybe I do love you,' she admitted. 'Then again, maybe I don't. What if it's just lust? Or simply an infatuation? For pity's sake, Byron, I've only known you two weeks!'

'That was long enough for me. *Two days* was long enough for me. But I can see how the time factor bothers you, so what I propose is this…'

Cleo rolled her eyes.

'Now, now, none of that. I'm not going to propose marriage again. Not yet. All I'm asking is for you to give me three months to prove to you that we genuinely love each other and will be happy together. Obviously, I need some time to show you that I am nothing like your first husband. I'm not interested at all in controlling you, my darling. I love that you have your own career, and I love how independent you are. I love your strength of character and your integrity. I especially love that you're not jumping at the chance to marry me. Trust me when I say I love that about you most of all. So, what do you say, Cleo? Would three months do it?'

'Three months,' she repeated slowly, somewhat stunned by all his compliments.

'I think that's long enough, don't you?' he prodded.

'I… I guess so…'

He smiled. 'Good. That's settled, then.' He stood up abruptly and strode around behind Scott's desk, pulling Cleo up into his arms and hugging her tightly. She didn't object, which he took as a good sign. So he kissed her.

She didn't object to that, either.

CHAPTER TWENTY-SIX

Friday night. Three months and one day later.

'TONIGHT...TONIGHT...!' CLEO sang as she put the finishing touches on her appearance.

Mungo howled at her feet, which made Cleo laugh.

'Yes, yes, I know,' she told him as she stroked the dog's head. 'Singing is not my forte.'

Fashion, however, was beginning to be something she excelled at, much to Cleo's surprise. She could hardly believe how good she'd become at choosing clothes that suited her, giving her the confidence to be seen with Byron, who was always elegantly dressed and far too handsome for words. Tonight's outfit was a purple woollen sheath with a matching thigh-length coat, teamed with seriously sexy black patent high heels. Her legs were housed in sleek stockings, whilst underneath she was wearing a black satin half-cup bra and a thong. Her hair was up, but softly, not severely. Her make-up was perfect and her perfume was a subtle but truly seductive scent with whispers of vanilla and musk.

Byron was taking her to some swanky restaurant in the city down near the quay where she just knew he was going to propose properly. And she was going to say yes without hesitation, the last three months having shown her that he was indeed the husband of her dreams. Not only considerate but truly kind, yet strong and sexy at the same time. The only place he tried to dominate her these days was sometimes in the bedroom, but she didn't mind that. She also gave as good as she got, at times surprising him with her own imaginative demands.

Frankly, she couldn't wait for Byron to ask her to marry him again.

The doorbell rang and her heart leapt. He was here, the man she adored, the man who was going to be her husband and the father of her children. They'd talked about children, Byron saying he wanted at least one, preferably two. Cleo had agreed with him that two was a good number.

Cleo hurried to answer the door, opening it with a ready smile on her face.

'Wow,' Byron said as he looked her up and down.

'And wow to you too,' she replied.

He was wearing black tonight, which was not a colour he usually wore. Black suit and an open-necked black shirt. Thankfully, no tie, or he might have looked like a gangster from a Hollywood movie. Not that he could, not with those beautiful blue eyes and blond hair.

'Very Quentin Tarantino,' she said, smiling.

Both of them loved their movies, and they talked about them endlessly, especially now that Byron had gone into partnership with Blake Randall. Cleo had been wary of meeting Blake at first—his reputation for being difficult had preceded him—but she had found him quite charming, once you got past the brooding façade he liked to project. He'd invited them both to visit him at his new Hollywood home, once he actually bought one, an invitation which they eagerly accepted.

Life as Byron's wife was going to be exciting, Cleo thought.

'Are you ready to go? Will the dog be all right, left on his own?'

Cleo frowned. 'How did you know he'd be on his own?'

Byron just shrugged. 'It's Friday night. Harvey usually takes Doreen out on a Friday night.'

'Not always. But he did tonight. Anyway, Mungo doesn't mind being left alone, as long as I leave the TV on and plenty of food and water. I took him out for a walk earlier so he'll be fine till Doreen gets home.'

Byron grinned. 'Are you assuming you're going to be later home than Doreen?'

'I was hoping not to be home at all!'

'You saucy minx! I suppose you think I'm going to propose tonight as well.'

Cleo experienced a moment's panic until she accepted he was only teasing her.

'If you don't, I think I'll be home *earlier* than Doreen.'

Byron laughed. 'Lock up, then. We have a big night ahead of us.'

Cleo was chatting happily away in the car when she realised they'd bypassed the inner city and were heading for the Eastern suburbs. 'Where are we going?'

'Just taking you somewhere private and romantic so that I can propose. Then we'll go eat and celebrate.'

'What if I say no?' she teased.

'You won't,' came his confident reply.

'Have you bought that ring I liked?' She'd pointed one out in a shop window one Sunday afternoon when they'd been strolling through the city.

'No.'

'Why not?'

'It was too cheap. You deserved something better.'

'Oh,' she said, her heart singing.

'Here we are.'

Cleo stared when they pulled into the driveway of a huge harbourside mansion. The large iron gates in the high security wall were locked but swung slowly open after Byron pressed a remote.

'This is Dad's place.'

'I thought he sold it.'

'He has. But the settlement's not until tomorrow. He gave me permission to come here tonight. There's a glorious view from the back terrace. Just the place to ask the woman I adore to marry me.'

'Oh, stop, please. If you keep saying things like that I'm going to cry.'

'Absolutely not. It'll ruin your make-up, and the photos.'

'Photos?'

'Selfies, then. With the Opera House and the bridge in the background.'

Cleo gaped as Byron drove through the gates and up to the wide front steps. The two-storeyed house wasn't as big as a palace, but it was palatial, with marble columns on the portico and an aristocratic front garden. All trimmed hedges and gravel pathways, and cleverly placed shade trees under which sat carved stone benches.

'Is your father selling the place fully furnished?' she asked on the way through the main living area, stunned at the furniture. And the decor. And everything. This house was every woman's dream come true.

'What? Oh, yes. Yes, he is.'

'Whoever bought it must be very rich.'

'He is.' Byron led her out onto the back terrace where the view was, indeed, glorious. So was the pool, plus a very cute pool house, beyond which the lawns sloped gently down to the water's edge.

'At last,' Byron said with a deep sigh, startling Cleo when he actually sank down on one knee in front of her. The small velvet box he drew out of his pocket was black. Byron flipped it open and Cleo's eyes glistened with happy tears. Not because the diamond ring was big and beautiful and expensive, but because of what it meant.

'Will you do me the honour of becoming my wife, darling Cleo?' he asked, his voice trembling slightly.

'Yes, of course I will,' she replied, wiping away her tears.

He stood up and took the ring from the box, slipping it onto her finger, the one that was now empty, Cleo having taken off her other wedding ring weeks ago. The ring fitted perfectly, the way *they* fitted perfectly.

'So, you like this house?' he asked as she stood there, wiggling her hand so that the solitaire diamond sparkled and flashed.

Cleo smiled. 'It's a magnificent house.'

'It's ours,' he said. 'Yours and mine. I'm the one who bought it. Dad wanted to give it to me but I've never been fond of nepotism, or in getting something I haven't earned.'

'But it must have cost you a fortune!' Cleo protested, her head whirling.

'It did. But it's a good investment. Even if we lose everything else we'll still have this to fall back on. And each other.'

'Oh, Byron. You are so good to me.'

He grinned. 'You deserve the very best. And I can afford to give it to you.'

She slapped him playfully on the arm. 'You are an arrogant beast. But I wouldn't have you any other way.'

They kissed. Then they kissed again. Cleo was away in another world when someone tapped her on the shoulder.

She spun around, startled to see Lloyd Maddox and his very beautiful new wife standing there with wide smiles on their faces.

'Sorry to interrupt, folks,' Lloyd said, his voice tinged with a slight American accent. 'But the people squashed into the pool house are getting antsy. Do you think they could come out and start the party now?'

Cleo stared at him, then up at Byron. 'You organised a surprise engagement party?'

'I did. Okay, everyone!' he called out. 'You can come out now.'

They spilled out loudly, offering congratulations and hugs with considerable volume. Everyone she and Byron cared about was there. Doreen and Harvey. Scott and Sarah. Grace and her husband. Rosalind and Lara. There was Blake Randall and his latest girlfriend, plus people she didn't recognise but who obviously knew Byron well. Everyone snapped photos of the happy couple on their phones, Cleo soon feeling a little faint from lack of food.

As if on cue, from out of the house materialised smartly dressed waiters who smoothly served drinks and finger food, which were both delicious and satisfying. Cleo suspected that Gloria was somewhere behind the scenes, organising everything.

'I still can't believe Byron bought this house for me,' Cleo said to Sarah when the two women got a chance to speak alone.

'So I heard. It's a fantastic place. Scott and I are still house-hunting, as you know. We were thinking of the Northern beaches but now that you'll be living here, I think we might buy somewhere close.'

They'd become good friends, all four of them, despite Byron not investing in McAllister Mines. Though he'd offered Scott a cash loan if he ever needed it.

'Oh, I'd love that,' Cleo said.

'How soon do you think you'll get married?' Sarah asked.

'Pretty soon, I think. Byron's been patient enough.'

'Please make it *very* soon if you want me to be your matron of honour. I'm having twins.'

'No!'

'Yes! I've known for a while but didn't want to say anything until my sixteen-week ultrasound when I knew everything was fine.'

'Goodness. What are they? Are they identical?'

'No. Not identical. A boy and a girl.'

'Wow. A complete family in one strike.'

'That's what Scott said. But I want more than two children. I want at least six.'

'Goodness!'

'That's what Scott said, too.'

'What did Scott say?' Byron asked as he joined them, winding an affectionate arm around Cleo's waist and drawing her close.

'Sarah's having twins,' Cleo told him. 'A boy and a girl.'

His stiffening was infinitesimal, but it was there, Cleo realising then just how much Byron wanted children. She wanted them too, but it was an even stronger need with him, one which she could hopefully satisfy. She was, however, older than Sarah at nearly thirty. If she wanted to give Byron children she would have to get moving. And soon.

It was well after midnight before the party broke up and the house was finally empty. Byron showed her through all the rooms she hadn't already seen, leading her up the grand marble staircase to the guest bedrooms, and, finally, into the master suite, which had its own private balcony and an even better view than downstairs.

'I love this house,' she said, turning to him. 'I was thinking, I won't be needing my home once we're married. I'd like to give it to Doreen. Then Harvey can come and live with her and Mungo.'

'Sounds like a good plan.'

'I have another plan, which I think is just as good.'

'Do tell.'

'From tonight, I don't want you to use protection.'

Byron's blue eyes flared wide. 'Are you serious?'

'Very.'

'Now that's an even better plan,' Byron said, and scooped her up into his arms.

* * *

When they married, two months later, Cleo was already pregnant. With a girl, they later discovered.

Harvey and Doreen were married just before Christmas, tying the knot in a simple register office wedding, and Mungo was a very happy dog when Harvey moved in permanently. He could con Harvey into a walk much more easily than Doreen.

Sarah's twins were born one month early on the twenty-sixth of January. Australia Day. They called the boy Edward, after Scott's father. And the girl Abigail, simply because Sarah liked the name.

Byron and Cleo's daughter was born four months later, and they called her April.

* * * * *

If you enjoyed
THE TYCOON'S OUTRAGEOUS PROPOSAL
why not explore the first part of Miranda Lee's
MARRYING A TYCOON duet?
THE MAGNATE'S TEMPESTUOUS MARRIAGE

Also by Miranda Lee, the
RICH, RUTHLESS AND RENOWNED *trilogy!*
THE ITALIAN'S RUTHLESS SEDUCTION
THE BILLIONAIRE'S RUTHLESS AFFAIR
THE PLAYBOY'S RUTHLESS PURSUIT
All available now!

#3565 UNDONE BY THE BILLIONAIRE DUKE
by Caitlin Crews

Eleanor Andrews refuses to see gorgeous Hugo, Duke of Grovesmoor, as anything but her boss! Hugo might be jaded and cynical, but innocent Eleanor fires his blood—and he can't turn down the challenge to unbutton his uptight employee!

#3566 HIS MAJESTY'S TEMPORARY BRIDE
The Princess Seductions
by Annie West

Cat Dubois's life as an illegitimate royal hasn't been luxurious. But when her princess half sister disappears ahead of her engagement to King Alexander, Cat agrees to step in! She didn't anticipate Alex's electric attraction—and Cat cannot hold back from his caress...

#3567 BOUND BY THE MILLIONAIRE'S RING
The Sauveterre Siblings
by Dani Collins

Millionaire Ramon Sauveterre will do anything to keep the spotlight off his family. Including faking an engagement to his head of PR, Isidora Garcia! She never forgave Ramon for breaking her heart. But resisting Ramon's heated touch proves utterly impossible!

#3568 THE VIRGIN'S SHOCK BABY
One Night With Consequences
by Heidi Rice

Megan never expected her plan to discover Dario De Rossi's business plans would lead to his bed! When Megan is violently punished, he's honor bound to protect her. But Megan has amnesia, believes they're in love...and she's carrying his baby!

YOU CAN FIND MORE INFORMATION ON UPCOMING HARLEQUIN® TITLES, FREE EXCERPTS AND MORE AT WWW.HARLEQUIN.COM.

HPCNM0917RB

SPECIAL EXCERPT FROM

◆ HARLEQUIN™

Presents®

Charlotte Adair has spent her life locked away—but once freed, she finds the one man she's ever loved, billionaire Rafe Costa, is now blind, believes she betrayed him and is bent on a vengeful seduction! Weeks after their scorching encounter he learns she's pregnant—with twins! Rafe steals Charlotte away, but she is a far from biddable prisoner. She is irresistible, defiant...and Rafe must seduce her into compliance!

Read on for a sneak preview of
Maisey Yates's book
THE ITALIAN'S PREGNANT PRISONER,
the final part of her
ONCE UPON A SEDUCTION... trilogy.

Charlotte hadn't touched a man since Rafe. She'd had no interest.

She needed to find some interest. Because she was going to have a normal life. Whatever she did, it would be her choice. And that was the point.

She didn't know what answers she had expected to find here. Right now, the only clear answer seemed to be that her body, her heart, was still affected by him.

He excused himself from the group, and suddenly he was walking her way. And she froze. Like a deer caught in the headlights. Or rather, like a woman staring at Rafe Costa.

She certainly wasn't the only woman staring. He moved with fluid grace, and if she didn't know better, she would never have known his sight was impaired at all.

He was coming closer, and as he did her heart tripped over itself, her hands beginning to shake. She wished she could touch him.

Oh, she wanted it more than anything. In that moment, she wanted it more than her next breath. To put her hands on Rafe Costa's face one more time. To kiss those lips again. To place her hand over his chest and see if she could still make his heart race.

It was easy to forget that her stepmother had told her how Rafe had left, taking an incentive offered by her father to end his tenure there earlier. It was easy to forget that and remember instead the way it had felt when he had kissed her. Touched her. The way she had pleaded with him to take her virginity, to make her his in every way.

Really, he had never wanted her. He had simply been toying with her.

She should remember that. Her treacherous, traitorous body should remember that well. But it didn't. Instead it was fluttering. As if a host butterflies had been set loose inside her.

Suddenly, he was there. So close that if she wanted to she could reach out and touch the edge of his sleeve with her fingertips.

Could bump into him accidentally, just to make contact. He wouldn't know it was her. He couldn't.

Suddenly, he turned. He was looking past her, his dark eyes unseeing, unfocused. But then he reached out and unerringly grabbed hold of her wrist, dragging her toward his muscular body.

"Charlotte."

Don't miss
THE ITALIAN'S PREGNANT PRISONER,
available October 2017 wherever
Harlequin Presents® books and ebooks are sold.

HARLEQUIN

Presents.

Coming next month—*Bound by the Millionaire's Ring*, the third part of Dani Collins's The Sauveterre Siblings quartet! Angelique, Henri, Ramon and Trella make up the world's most renowned family—wherever they go, scandal is sure to follow. They're protected by the best security money can buy, but what happens when each of these Sauveterre siblings meets the one person who can breach their heart?

The Sauveterre playboy is about to acquire a temporary fiancée...

Millionaire race-car driver Ramon Sauveterre is no stranger to fame, but he'll do just about anything to keep the spotlight off his family. Including faking an engagement to his gorgeous head of PR, Isidora Garcia!

Isidora cannot forgive Ramon for dragging her into this farce— just as she'll never forgive him for the indiscretion that broke her heart. But while their relationship might be a deception, the burning longing his kisses spark is all too real—and resisting Ramon's heated touch until the end of their arrangement proves utterly impossible!

Bound by the Millionaire's Ring
Available October 2017!

Pursued by the Desert Prince
His Mistress with Two Secrets
Available now!

And don't miss the final part—Trella and Xavier's story— available January 2018!

HP06107

Want to give in to temptation with
steamy tales of irresistible desire?

Check out **Harlequin® Presents®,
Harlequin® Desire** and
Harlequin® Kimani™ Romance books!

New books available every month!

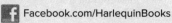

CONNECT WITH US AT:

Harlequin.com/Community

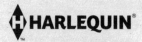

Facebook.com/HarlequinBooks

Twitter.com/HarlequinBooks

Instagram.com/HarlequinBooks

Pinterest.com/HarlequinBooks

ReaderService.com

H HARLEQUIN®

**ROMANCE WHEN
YOU NEED IT**

PGENRE2017